# AN ENCHANTED MOMENT...

He held her close as her arms stole around his neck.
Feeling her soft cheek brush past his chin, he tilted
her head and bent to kiss her. Slowly, his hands moved
to caress her, sending shivers over her body as she felt
the full power of the passion flaring between them. And
instantly all her fears were forgotten in the splendor of
her love. . . .

### SIGNET Books by Glenna Finley

(More Glenna Finley titles in the back of this book.)

---

**To order these titles,
please use coupon on the
last page of this book.**

# TIMED FOR LOVE

by
Glenna Finley

*Love, all alike, no season knowes, nor clyme,
Nor houres, dayes, moneths, which are the
rags of time.*

—JOHN DONNE

A SIGNET BOOK
**NEW AMERICAN LIBRARY**
TIMES MIRROR

Based in part on *Nurse Pro Tem* by Glenna Finley
© 1967 by Arcadia House

 SIGNET TRADEMARK REG. U.S. PAT. OFF. AND FOREIGN COUNTRIES
REGISTERED TRADEMARK—MARCA REGISTRADA
HECHO EN CHICAGO, U.S.A.

SIGNET, SIGNET CLASSICS, MENTOR, PLUME AND MERIDIAN BOOKS
are published by The New American Library, Inc.,
1301 Avenue of the Americas, New York, New York 10019

First Signet Printing, August, 1979

1  2  3  4  5  6  7  8  9

PRINTED IN THE UNITED STATES OF AMERICA

# Chapter One

❧ ❧ ❧

There was nothing unusual about that late August day in Manhattan, nothing in the midday quiet to indicate an impending calamity in the studios of the Continental Broadcasting Company.

A lazy housefly was circling over the traffic desk in the International Division at the time, and the summer air was suffocatingly close and humid. Even the clatter of the teletype machines on the far wall of the big room was muted and sporadic—as if the news they transmitted was hardly worth the effort.

The atmosphere changed abruptly when the actual confrontation between Joshua Blake and Jane Chapin took place. He was a tall man in his mid-thirties who came through the main door and marched purposefully past desks left deserted by the lunch exodus, straight toward the corner of the room where Jane was sitting.

"Good afternoon," he said, putting his attaché case

down on the corner of her desk with a decisive motion. "I'd like to see Mr. Hall, please."

She had been concentrating on prying up the lid of a container of iced coffee, but she raised her head long enough to say, "I'm sorry—you can't. They should have told you upstairs that it was a waste of time."

His bored expression vanished, and he directed a frowning gaze at her bent head. "Would you look at me long enough to repeat that," he commanded.

The lid was finally off and put aside.

"I said that it's no go," Jane Chapin repeated in a kind but distinct voice. "You might just as well buzz off and find a more receptive desk for that briefcase." Then she paused to survey the drops of spilled coffee. "Wouldn't you think that just once I could do it properly?"

"Obviously your talents lie in other areas. If you can tear yourself away from the earthshaking procedure of opening that damned cup of coffee—why can't I see Mr. Hall?"

"There's no need," she replied, aware that the temperature between them had dropped perceptibly. "The position has been filled. He interviewed a new page this morning, so opportunity's already knocked and the game's over. They were supposed to tell you upstairs so you wouldn't make the trip down here for nothing, but the personnel office is one of those places where the left hand doesn't know what the right—"

"For pete's sake, will you shut up!" He shot her a baleful look. "Now, sort it all out and start over again. It might be easier if you tried a moment of silence first."

Jane pushed back a strand of sandy hair that had more than a hint of red in it and surveyed him deliberately. Her glance slithered from his firmly brushed dark brown hair to a forceful jaw line, roved over the immaculate white shirt collar and went back again to a pair of cold brown eyes. Then, still taking her time, she rubbed the top of her nose, leaving an erratic smudge of coffee. "Is there a time limit on this game?" she asked, pursing her lips provocatively. "Remember the old saying, 'there is a time to keep silence and a time to speak.' "

"I remember another one—'rude is never funny.' " He shot an impatient look at the office behind her. "You certainly aren't Mr. Hall's secretary."

Her trim figure stiffened at his innuendo and she smoothed the collar of her emerald linen blouse as if she needed time to keep her temper under control. "No," she said finally, "I'm Jane Chapin. Not Mr. Hall's secretary—nor the traffic manager, who also happens to be out," she added, intercepting his frowning glance at the nameplate on the desk. "However, Mr. Hall's secretary asked me to deliver the word to any men who might appear." Jane's glance flicked upward again. "Quite frankly, I should think you'd be a little old for a page job anyway."

"I couldn't agree with you more." His voice was grim. "I'm Josh Blake and I had an appointment with Mr. Hall."

"Oh . . . oh." Her lips twitched upward slightly. "I'm afraid you're too late. He went out the back door a few minutes ago. Incidentally, I hope I didn't deflate you by mentioning the page job. Quite a few older men—"

"Don't bother to explain," he cut in, raking his hand through his hair. "I hadn't realized that I'd turned gray overnight. Perhaps I could leave a note for Mr. Hall before senility sets in."

"Of course." She started to offer him a pen as he was reaching for a scratch pad on the desk.

The inevitable collision took place beside her still-full

container of coffee, which promptly overturned, spewing the contents over the corner of the desk where he was leaning.

There was a stricken moment of arrested movement. Then, slowly, Blake moved away from the desk, rested his case on a nearby chair, and grimly set about staunching his suit with an immaculate handkerchief.

"Isn't it fortunate that there's no cream," Jane said in a subdued voice, "and that the brown of your suit almost matches."

"And that it's a warm day so that I needn't worry about catching cold." His words grated out savagely.

"Well, there's no need to be unpleasant. After all, it was an accident. Of course, your handkerchief is rather a mess, but I'll be happy to launder it for you."

"From that, good Lord, deliver me."

"I beg your pardon?"

"Never mind." He surveyed the soggy handkerchief he was clutching.

"Perhaps the wastebasket . . ." she suggested hesitantly.

"I think you're right." Trying to give her body as wide a berth as possible in the limited space, he walked behind her desk and dropped the limp tan ball into the wastebasket.

Jane, too, was clearly chary of a physical encounter, and she rose from the swivel chair to move out of his way. As she did, her linen skirt brushed his precariously placed briefcase and knocked it on the floor. "Oh, I'm sorry," she apologized. "Let me—"

His arm shot out and held her away. "Don't bother. The way this farce is going, we'd be sure to bump heads. So if you'll just oblige me by standing still. . . ." He put her firmly against a filing cabinet and bent swiftly to retrieve his property.

4

As she came into contact with the side of the steel cabinet, the top filing drawer dislodged. Jane watched with undisguised horror as it slid out directly over his unsuspecting head.

"Oh, don't!" she squeaked.

"What's the matter?" he asked, straightening automatically.

"Stay down!" She tried to arrest his upward movement and thereby was privileged to look him eye-to-eye as his head came into contact with the bottom of the steel drawer.

His dark eyes closed abruptly at the collision and he sank onto his knees. A faint moan escaped his lips.

"I'm so sorry." Jane slammed the drawer shut and knelt beside him. "It happened so quickly. Are you all right?" There was no mistaking her concern.

"I'll—be—fine." His hand groped for a chair and he pulled himself up.

"If you'll come into the next room, there's a couch where you can lie down and rest."

"That won't be necessary." His voice gained strength as he leaned against the partition of Hall's executive office. The color was gradually coming back into his lean tanned face. "Look," he said reasonably, "why don't you just go away and leave me alone."

"But I'd like to help."

"I don't think I could survive any more of your help, thanks."

Rebuffed by his obvious scorn, she backed against the desk. "Of course, Mr. Blake. I'll tell Mr. Hall you were in."

He reached stiffly for his case. "Thank you. I'll call him later to set up another appointment. Sometime"—his glance was baleful—"when his secretary is here."

For a moment, their gaze held. Though there wasn't a word spoken, the gauntlet was so obviously thrown at her feet that she almost consciously stepped over it when she moved around the corner of the desk.

"I hope you won't have too bad a headache from this," she commented.

He turned toward the door. "There are headaches and headaches."

"I meant the one caused by the drawer." Her voice pursued him sweetly.

He bestowed a final discouraging look over his shoulder. "I don't expect that one to bother me at all."

On his way out, he paused just long enough to hold the door for a young man of medium height who was coming in.

The newcomer had a hawklike face with black hair brushed sleekly back from it and dark eyes which smiled down on Jane as he approached the traffic desk. "*¡Hola, chiquita! ¿Qué tal?*"

"Greetings to you, Tomás, my friend." She returned his smile. "How is International's esteemed traffic manager?"

"The traffic manager is fine. The graduate student isn't so great." He perched on a corner of the desk and watched her gather some papers together. "I feel more like a hundred and six than twenty-six today."

"What's the matter—trouble with your thesis?" she asked sympathetically.

"Not really. Oh, hell! I don't know." His features suddenly pulled together in a fierce frown. "Sometimes I think I'm crazy to spend time trying to get a master's degree."

"But Tommy, you know that's what you decided to do."

"I know that there's no future on this traffic desk and

6

that there isn't any opening for me in the domestic side of the network right now." He rolled a pencil back and forth aimlessly on the desktop as he spoke. "But I still wonder if going for a degree is worth the effort. Besides, if my marketing prof has his way, I can kiss the five credits on that course good-bye."

"I've heard that talk before." She grinned at him as she picked up an armful of typed reports. "This is only your second quarter and somehow you're still going along just fine. Have courage, Tomasino."

"But that prof honestly does seem to have a down on me."

"Then turn on some Irish blarney, Mr. Carmichael, and charm him the way you do the rest of us around here. Anyone who can keep peace among twenty-five South American and ten Mid-East radio people in this place—plus assorted Europeans—should find one marketing professor a real piece of cake." She gave the desktop a hasty scrutiny to make sure she hadn't forgotten anything. "I'd better go back to the dispensary and get on with the inventory before those supplies are moved upstairs."

"I thought you'd finished with that."

"It takes time. Some of those drawers haven't been opened in years. At any moment, I expect to run into green mold from an early experiment by Dr. Pasteur. No wonder Mr. Hall decided to use that office space for something else." She looked at her watch. "It'll take me the rest of the afternoon to inventory the drug cabinet."

"Something upset you?" He hung his coat on a nearby rack and started turning back the cuffs of his blue oxford-cloth shirt.

"Not something—someone."

"You mean the efficient-looking fellow who nearly ran me down at the door?"

7

"None other."

Tom Carmichael gave her a mocking glance. "What had you been doing to him? There was a frantic gleam in his eye."

"Pain and desperation, I imagine. You saw a man on the edge of the inferno," she said, gesturing extravagantly. "A man who was afraid his foot might slip and plunge him back into the abyss."

"With an imagination like yours, you should be a full-time scriptwriter."

"The gentleman who was hurrying out the door wouldn't agree with you. He has a very low opinion of my talents."

"Seriously, Janie, what was the trouble?"

She shrugged. "Put it down in your program log that the gentleman and I agreed to disagree."

"Then he's crazy," Tom said in a satisfyingly definite tone. "You're the best damned departmental coordinator we've ever had."

She smiled and wrinkled her nose at him. "That's a lot of title for a glorified cleaning woman, secretary, coffee-maker . . ."

". . . who somehow manages to pull everything together in this crazy place," Tom finished. "Things never worked so well as they have since you agreed to give Mr. Hall a hand."

"Anybody can clear out cupboards. As soon as I arrange to send the last of this medical stuff up to the network section, I'll be doing some other fascinating things for him—like setting up work schedules for the Spanish section."

Tom refused to be led astray by her disclaimer. "You can say what you like, but everybody around here agrees that Mr. Hall knew what he was doing when he convinced you to join the staff—even on a temporary basis."

"That's because most of the announcers were bored with the scenery. Any new face was welcome. Or figure," she added darkly. "And if that new Mexican announcer doesn't keep his hands to himself when I walk past his desk the next time, I'm going to violate the State Department's nonaggression pact."

"He's just enthusiastic," Tom said nonchalantly. "And he isn't the only one. You can't tell me that our revered network medico wanted to discuss foreign policy when he came and took you out to dinner last night."

Her eyebrows rose. "Dr. Jamieson mainly wanted to check on the supply inventory that we'll be transferring to his section." Jane's blue eyes then gleamed with laughter as she turned to go. "He was curious about how many Florence Nightingale capes were stored away, how many silver lamps—that sort of thing."

"Uh-huh, I'll bet." Tom delayed her to have a final word. "I'd like to hear another editorial opinion on that. From what I've heard, Mark Jamieson isn't a man to waste his time on ancient history. He's a real tiger about wanting the very best in equipment and staff for his department upstairs."

At that very moment, there was a discussion being held in the medical section a few floors above which confirmed Tom's opinion.

Dr. Mark Jamieson, a sturdy, fair-haired man in his mid-thirties, was perched on the corner of his desk talking to the network personnel chief about Continental's new employee. "You can forget about trying to convince Jane Chapin to stick around," he was telling the other man. "I used my best arguments last night and it was no dice."

"How about an offer to put her in front of the cameras

on the network side," the personnel man said, grinning. "I'm not the only one around here who likes sandy-haired beauties packaged just right. Especially a woman who's intelligent in the bargain, so she doesn't trade on those other assets."

"I know," the doctor responded. "But when I asked if she wouldn't like to come to work in my section after her stint with the International Division is over, she just started shaking her head. She was polite, even interested in hearing about my virus research—"

"And?"

"And the answer was still 'no.' That oil company she worked for in South America wants her to go to the Middle East later this year. Before that, she's planning a vacation at her family's place in the Northwest. Seems it's a ranch with horses, green rolling hills, and Mount Rainier in the background. By the time we got to coffee, I was asking if she didn't want a house guest."

The personnel man thought of his humid subway ride home. "If she changes her mind and takes you along," he said, "tell her that you have a friend."

It was considerably later that afternoon when the object of their discussion was finally able to sit down at her desk and stretch out a pair of admirable legs to relax. Madge Waverly, private secretary to the chief of the International Division, chose that moment to walk past. "You're pretty vulnerable in that position," she commented, pulling up.

Jane moved her shoes carefully on the edge of her wastebasket so she wouldn't upset it. "Putting your feet up has great therapeutic value. Besides, I've been typing that inventory for so long that I'm practically numb. I need all the help I can get."

"Where's all the production staff?" Madge asked, surveying the empty desks around them.

"Scattered like chaff on the wind." Jane reached for her purse as she went on to explain. "One producer's on vacation, one has the day off, and two are in the studios. I'm holding the fort for the moment."

"I wish you were holding down the same fort permanently. You're worth two of those crazy characters."

"True, true," Jane agreed with a twinkle. "But don't tell me. Tell Mr. Hall or the payroll section."

"I can't tell Mr. Hall—at least, not now. He's busy with a visiting fireman." Madge lowered her voice conspiratorially. "If I were fifteen years younger, I wouldn't be wasting time out here talking to you."

"Okay, I'll bite. What would you be doing, Miss Waverly?"

"I'd be sitting at my desk looking decorative when the fireman leaves. The rumor is that he's been sent up from our Washington legal section to assist Mr. Hall and make sure that we're broadcasting the approved material to *Sud-América*. How's my pronunciation?"

"Terrible," Jane said absently. "Watch the a's."

Madge grimaced in mock irritation. "I knew everybody in this department had a better accent than mine, but I never thought it would include the temporary help as well."

Jane laughed and pushed a strand of hair from her forehead. "I've spent almost as much time speaking Spanish as I have English. My dad was a petroleum geologist, and we once lived next door to the Halls in South America when I was growing up. That's the main reason Mr. Hall hired me now. When I stopped by to say hello to him, I thought I was just passing through New York."

"Well, he was delighted to find you even temporarily at

loose ends," Madge said. "You don't have a chance of escaping 'til your six weeks are up."

"Not if I wanted Mr. Hall to buy my lunch that day," Jane agreed, laughing. "Even then, it wouldn't have worked if Dr. Jamieson hadn't told him about an apartment being sublet just that week."

"How do you like it?"

"The apartment? Fine, for a short term. The furnishings are a little weird, but my absentee landlady is a singing coach for grand opera, so she's entitled to some eccentricities." Jane shrugged and went on, "Actually, it doesn't matter. I've moved so much in my life."

"All twenty-four or twenty-five years of it," Madge put in with a tolerant glance.

"Well, it seems as if I've been living out of a suitcase forever," Jane concluded wistfully. "That was why I'd been looking forward to going home on this leave. But working in International has been fun—the people are marvelous." She started searching through her purse, methodically piling the contents onto her desk. "Somewhere in here, I have a lipstick." Sunglasses, wallet, credit card holder, and stick cologne mounted in an unsteady array.

"For heaven's sake, what are you doing with a tea bag?" Madge asked.

"I can't imagine. I only wish I'd discovered it before now. Most of it's scattered over the bottom of my bag."

"I'd better get back to work," the older woman said with a look at her watch.

"Why hurry? The legal watchdog's probably still holding forth."

"That's all right. I want to be around when he leaves. He's tall with a sort of lean and hungry look."

"Maybe he missed lunch. . . ."

Madge ignored her. "Dark brown eyes that look

through you politely. Austere but considerate—you know the type."

"I haven't heard of that type since I stopped reading fairy tales."

"Heavens, what's soured your disposition?"

"I have a suspicion that we're going to get a touch of managed news," Jane said wryly. "Frederick Hall has never needed any help with this department before, and it seems a shame to undermine his authority now. I don't see why the higher-ups on the domestic side can't leave well enough alone. Instead, they have to send one of their Washington lawyers with State Department connections to smooth our way."

Madge's eyebrow rose in amusement. "Why the soapbox?"

"Put it down to living around too many Caribbean and South American dictators. I have a built-in dislike of efficiency experts, cocktail circuit lotharios, and State Department statisticians."

"My word, you're touchy today. Sight unseen with the man, too."

A flush crept up under Jane's delicate cheekbones and she kept her eyes studiously on the desktop as Madge looked at the time again. "Well, I'd better get back to my desk," the secretary said. "Their meeting will be breaking up any minute. Mr. Hall has an appointment with some Pan American Union men uptown in fifteen minutes. Oh, hello, Horrie." She greeted the sandy-haired, middle-aged man who vibrated rather than walked through the doorway.

" 'lo, Madge. *Buenas tardes, rojita linda.*"

Jane smiled absently up at him as he paused, fidgeting, by her desk. "Hi, Horrie. How did your show go?"

The International production chief snorted. "How do

you suppose it went with a twirp like that new Portuguese announcer?"

"What happened?"

"First off, he started to make the network break without hitting the button on the control panel, so I hissed at him to pick up the cable. Do you know what the damn fool did?"

Both women shook their heads.

"He began looking around the floor of the studio for an electrical connection. I ask you!"

Madge laughed without sympathy. "You shouldn't have expected anything else. Poor man! The others in the section probably didn't take time to explain your vocabulary."

"I'm glad you said didn't take time rather than didn't have time," Horrie Cole said petulantly. "According to my time studies, that group has more spare time than any other language section."

"I know, I know," Madge said, breaking into his tirade. "And so does Mr. Hall—so there's no use taking up his time with it."

"Somebody around here should be interested in a little more efficiency," Cole muttered.

"Somebody is," Jane put in wickedly. "Haven't you heard, Horrie? A brand-spanking-new efficiency expert is in talking with Mr. Hall now. I'll bet he'd be fascinated with your time studies on the various language groups." She ignored Madge's violent gestures behind Horrie Cole's back and went on. "He might even want to incorporate them in his final report."

"Do you think so?" Cole's pale blue eyes flickered behind sandy lashes. "I can see where this might be a break. Perhaps I'd better unearth that folio I did on comparison time studies in the Spanish and Portuguese sections last spring." He started to move off toward his office door. "That's a whale of an idea, Jane. Maybe I'll finally get some recognition on my work."

Madge looked at Jane severely. "As a motion study man, he's a dandy international radio man and you know it, my pet. I hope you're around to pick up the pieces when our expert bats him down. Oh-oh, there's Mr. Hall's door opening now. I'd better get back to work. See you later."

Jane unhurriedly started to clear the contents of her purse from her desk. She kept her head averted as Frederick Hall's side office door closed noisily and footsteps approached.

"Jane, you're still here. I'm glad we found you in."

She raised her head and gazed solemnly up at the two men standing by her desk. If I'd one iota of sense, she thought, I would have stayed out of sight. Aloud, she merely said, "Can I help you, Mr. Hall?"

The aquiline features of the older man had softened as he looked down at her. Thinning gray hair was brushed neatly back from his high, narrow forehead, and a sober gray and white seersucker suit emphasized the frailty of his slender frame. Only the direct gaze of his bright blue eyes made one realize that the vapid appearance, the fussy, precise approach, might effectively shade an astuteness that became evident on longer acquaintance.

The irony is, Jane thought, that all of us in International could tell the powers that be what a wonderful man Frederick Hall is, but he'll never put up the slightest defense of his own. He just sits in meetings and lets the officious souls sell him down the river. Well, he might be going down the river, she decided, but the assured man beside him was going to find it rough paddling in the current, as well. "Can I help you with something, Mr. Hall?" she repeated quietly.

He beamed down at her. "No need to be so formal, my dear. Jane, this is Joshua Blake. Mr. Blake, I'd like to present Jane Chapin, our departmental coordinator and an honorary niece of mine. Her father and I have been friends for more years than I like to remember."

"How do you do, Miss Chapin."

It seemed to Jane that there was a world of coolness in Blake's tone. Evidently their previous encounter was to be ignored.

"Mr. Blake." Her acknowledgment was equally abrupt. They stared warily at each other without further conversation.

Frederick Hall's benevolent beam changed to one of uneasy regard at the sudden silence. Nervously, he shuffled some of the papers he was carrying. "Jane—if you aren't too busy, could you show Mr. Blake around the department?" He looked back to the younger man. "I'd do it myself if I didn't have an appointment uptown."

"I understand, Mr. Hall." Blake's calm words filled the breach smoothly. "You've been very generous with your time already."

"Don't be silly, man." Frederick Hall's thin shoulders straightened with effort. "Quite frankly, I didn't think too much of the idea of a Washington watchdog when the idea was first brought up. Jane will remember my reaction." He smiled at her. "But perhaps it's for the best, after all. Those ideas of yours on extra programs for the west coast of South America might get the response we've been wanting."

"I hope so, sir."

The prig, thought Jane violently, the insufferable, pompous prig!

"Yes, indeed," Hall went on. "Well, I must be off. Jane, just take Mr. Blake on a general tour around the department. He'll be occupying that empty office which belonged to Carvajal, our former Spanish department head." Hall turned to Blake and explained, "The man we have now prefers a desk out with the people in his section. His name is Emilio Forcada. You'll meet him a little later on. Right now, he's off-duty unless—" He paused in mid-sentence and glanced at Jane in wry amusement.

Her nod answered his unspoken question. "It's possible we'll run into Señor Forcada in the music library," she said. "He's putting in some overtime these days."

"So I hear," the older man replied cryptically. "Well, I must get going. Jane—if you'll take over. I'll see you to-morrow, Mr. Blake."

"The name is Josh. . . ."

"That doesn't sound as formidable, does it?" Hall beamed on the two of them and gave a jerky gesture of farewell before he walked back to his office.

"Would you like to spend some time in your office, Mr. Blake, or would you like to look around the department first?" Jane finished clearing her desktop with a decisive air.

"The tour would be fine if it won't be taking you away from your work."

"Not at all. I was officially finished a half hour ago."

A small flicker of a smile appeared and was gone. "If you'd prefer, this could be allowed as legitimate overtime for company business. Shall we synchronize our watches to make it really official?"

"That won't be necessary, Mr. Blake."

"Then perhaps we should have an understanding, Miss Chapin."

"That won't be necessary, either."

"I think it is." He leaned negligently against the water cooler and stared down at her with a look which contained all the warmth he might bestow on a puppy whose manners were found lacking. "I gather you're a temporary employee so you feel you can be as rude as you like. Since Mr. Hall thinks highly of you, I can only conclude that your disagreeable manner is directed at me. Frankly, I'm getting sick and tired of it."

"What an elegant dressing down, Mr. Blake. Doesn't the defendant have any rights? Or are you accusing me of purposely overturning that container of coffee on you, as well?" She surveyed his suit deliberately. "I'm sorry that you had to go home and change, but you're quite safe now. There's nothing lethal left on my desk." She watched a red tinge spread under his well-defined cheekbones before she went on. "That file drawer has been the bane of the traffic desk for some time. Are you charging me with premeditated assault, or is that the proper legal terminology?"

A muscle in his cheek twitched. "If you're not careful, Miss Chapin," he said through clenched teeth, "the only premeditated assault will be of my doing." He straightened abruptly. "Shall we get on with the tour."

"Certainly, Mr. Blake." She moved smoothly past him. "You won't mind if I walk ahead of you?"

"The farther ahead the better," he muttered just loud enough to reach her ears.

She paused at the glass cubicle next to Frederick Hall's executive offices and gestured toward the man inside. "This is Mr. Cole, our production head. Horrie, may I present Joshua Blake, who's going to assist Mr. Hall."

Horrie Cole bounced happily up from behind his desk and leaned over to shake hands. "Happy to know you,

Blake. We've heard how you plan to streamline the operation here."

"That wasn't what I had in mind."

"Well, I suppose we could do with a little jacking up," Cole pursued the topic relentlessly. "You fellows from the domestic side are more practical about those things. As a matter of fact, I've always prided myself that I ran a pretty tight section."

"I'm sure you do," Josh muttered.

"It's sort of a hobby of mine," Horrie continued, lowering his solid frame to the corner of his desk. "I was just telling Jane about the time and motion studies I did for the Spanish and Portuguese sections and she thought you might be interested in seeing them."

"That was thoughtful of her," Blake said in a tone which meant nothing of the kind.

"You bet!" With his round cheeks, Horace Cole looked like an eager chipmunk who had unearthed his choice cache of nuts. "I think I took them home, but I'll scrounge around tonight and see if I can find them."

"That will be fine."

"And I'll check with you first thing tomorrow," Cole promised.

The tour resumed in silence. An elaborate silence. Jane detoured uneasily by the traffic desk.

"Ah, the scene of the crime," Josh said.

She ignored his comment. "Mr. Blake, this is Tom Carmichael, International's traffic manager."

"I'm glad to know you, Mr. Blake." Tom rose quickly from behind his desk and offered his hand. "Mr. Hall told me to give you any help you might need."

"Thanks very much. I'll appreciate it."

"You'll find Janie a help, too." Tom's hand came down

affectionately on her shoulder. "She knows more answers than most of us who've been in the department for years."

"I can well believe it."

Jane glanced up in suspicion at Blake's quiet comment, but he was looking at his watch.

"I think we'd better keep on with this tour," he said. "Nice to have met you, Carmichael. We'll get together later on to thrash out the program details."

"Right. How about it, Janie?" Tom asked. "Can you keep our date?"

"Probably. I shouldn't be much longer, so I'll meet you here." She gave him a smile and hurried off to catch up with her charge.

"I hope this isn't keeping you from something important," Blake said to her as they made their way through a battery of deserted desks and headed toward the main entrance of the department.

"Not at all," she said coolly. "I'm glad to be of help to Mr. Hall."

There might be very few sure things in the world, Jane decided, but one of them was her resolve to explain no further about her plans to join Tom after work at the favorite International meeting place across the street. It was a run-of-the-mill bar and grill favored by its customers for its wide leather booths and shadowy interior on the late summer days. If Joshua Blake happened to imagine that Tom's casual invitation held more significance than intended—that was all right, too. Certainly something seemed to be making his expression especially disapproving just then.

"I gather this section belongs to the Spanish announcers," he said, slowing his steps.

She nodded. "And writers. Most of them work the morning shift, although Emilio is probably still around."

"The head of the section?"

She nodded again and then gestured toward the far end of the long room, where a handful of men were busy at typewriters. "Those fellows comprise the English section. Right now, they're getting ready for their broadcasting time, so it probably wouldn't do to interrupt them. The Mideast section is next, but they work another shift. The rest of the empty desks down there belong to the few French and German people we have. International hasn't too much programming in those languages beamed to South America—just enough to serve the displaced Europeans who still cling to their native tongues. However, you're probably more familiar with their scheduling than I am."

"Ummm." He looked around the almost deserted room and then drummed his fingers on a nearby desktop. "What else is on the agenda?"

She led the way through the big main door. "Here on the left are the studios . . ." She looked up, hesitating.

"Let's not bother with them." His tone was abrupt. "A studio is the same anywhere. What else is there to see?"

"Around to the right, we have the music library." Her voice came over her shoulder. "They have one of the most comprehensive collections of South American music in this country. This is also where we keep the acetates of the current domestic shows which are going to be broadcast with a foreign language script."

They paused at the entrance of a hallway, perhaps twenty feet long, which had four doors opening from it.

"These go into the timing rooms," she explained. "The producers use the turntables there to find how long the various parts of their shows are running, and the writers use them to time the numbers for their musical shows. That way they can determine how much script is needed.

You'll notice that all the doors are heavy and sound-proof." She pushed hard on one and nodded for him to look over her shoulder into the deserted cubicle beyond. There were two record turntables with heavy, utilitarian playing arms mounted on a scarred tabletop. A metal chair with a thin padded plastic seat was pushed carelessly against one of the unadorned but soundproofed walls, while in the far corner a small table held a single glass ashtray overflowing with cigarette butts. Institutional gray linoleum covered the floor.

"It's hardly a candidate for *House Beautiful,*" was Blake's only comment.

"Evidently the network budget has never been stretched to give these rooms any extras, but no one seems to mind," she said, letting the heavy door fall shut behind them.

Their footsteps echoed on the floor as they moved over to a waist-high counter which divided the room in half. Behind it, metal shelves held row upon row of records in cardboard jackets. Popular and classical albums occupied one wall, and small aluminum ladders were conveniently spaced along each aisle to put the ceiling-high shelves within reach.

"The librarian's quarters are at the back," Jane said in a low voice, "and someone is always on duty when the International Division is on the air. Strange—I thought Anita was here this afternoon."

"Anita?"

"Anita Warren, the head librarian. It looks as if she's gone out, so we might as well leave, too." Jane turned from the counter and started toward the door.

A violent sneeze at the back of the room made them both turn in surprise. There was a short silence, then a muffled giggle, and finally, almost sheepishly, a couple emerged from one of the dim recesses.

"Well, honestly!" Jane's tone held a mixture of amusement and irritation. "Aren't you a little old for such shenanigans?"

"We were not playing hide and seek, *rojita linda,*" the tall man said, ushering his rather striking brunette companion up the narrow aisle before him. "Quite frankly, we hoped you'd go away."

"Thank you very much," Jane said, straightening perceptibly. "You'd better mind your manners."

"Nothing personal, Janie," said the tall, thin man, who smiled engagingly at her as he leaned on the counter. He had thick dark hair which brushed his collar, and a generous Roman nose. His companion was an attractive young woman who almost matched his height. A slim, black skirt hugged her hips more tightly than fashion decreed, and the white peasant blouse she wore clung provocatively low at the bodice.

Jane noticed Joshua Blake's stern mouth had relaxed into a frankly admiring smile and she felt a moment of pique. "Anita, may I present Mr. Blake," she said, trying not to show it.

"How do you do, Mr. Blake." Anita Warren's tone was demure, oddly at variance with the glance she bestowed under curling black lashes.

"Miss Warren . . ." he acknowledged politely.

"And the head of our Spanish section, Emilio Forcada." Jane directed her gaze at Forcada, who was looking unabashedly bored at the whole proceeding. "Mr. Blake is up from Washington to assist Mr. Hall."

Forcada's attention sharpened immediately. His arm slipped down from Anita Warren's shoulders and he straightened to full height. "You must forgive our little joke, Mr. Blake. At this time of day, we're not expecting . . ."

"Visiting firemen?"

Jane turned sharply to look at Blake as he murmured the phrase.

His dark eyes suddenly flicked her way, and his outward look of amusement deepened.

"My apologies, Señor Forcada." Blake's manner was easy. "Miss Chapin was good enough to show me around so I could get an idea of the department before starting to work in earnest tomorrow."

"Of course, of course, I understand." Forcada straightened a bright red bow tie that was pushed off center on his shirt collar and came around the end of the counter. "I was about to start timing a show I'm putting together." He put a firm hand under Blake's elbow. "Come along. I have all the material in this first timing room. You'll be interested in hearing it."

Blake lingered just long enough to give the two women a startled nod before going along with Forcada.

Jane smiled as she watched the cubicle door slam shut under the announcer's heavy hand.

Anita pursed her lips thoughtfully. "So that's the new man, eh? Madge said he was coming."

"The news gets around fast."

"When they look like Mr. Blake, it does," Anita said frankly. "Although I don't see why he had to monopolize Emilio."

"From my side of the arena," Jane said laughing, "I think it was the other way around. I hope that show Emilio is putting together is just a fifteen-minute one, or Mr. Blake will wish he'd packed a box lunch."

"You're right." Anita sighed and smoothed her skirt down on her hips. "Well, I suppose I'd better get to work.

My desk is piled with stuff to catalog." She gave Jane an absent nod and headed toward the back of the room.

Jane's smile deepened as she recalled that Anita never wasted time with a member of her own sex. Then she looked at her watch and a slight frown creased her brow. It was getting late and Tom was probably still waiting at his desk. She bit her lip in indecision and then she walked firmly up to the timing room door and pushed it open.

Wailing Latin trumpet music exploded in her ears like genii suddenly escaping from a stoppered bottle.

"Come in, *rojita,* come in," Forcada shouted over the din as he reached reluctantly for the volume control. The music tempered from a screech to a brassy background roar. "I was just telling Mr. Blake that you need sufficient volume to really appreciate music like this."

Jane noted amusedly that Joshua Blake was watching in stricken silence from the corner of the cubicle farthest away from the record player.

"This brass you get in Latin-American rhythms . . ." Forcada continued.

". . . Excuse me, Emilio," Jane cut in, stepping in front of him to turn the record down so that she could talk in a normal tone of voice. "I won't interrupt long—I just wanted to tell Mr. Blake that since he's in your good hands, I'll be going."

"But you can't—" Blake cut in desperately.

"Fine, *rojita.*" Forcada was terse. "I'll be glad to take care of Mr. Blake."

"Ah, there you are!" interrupted an enthusiastic voice from the doorway.

They turned to see Horrie Cole holding the door open with one hand while clutching an untidy stack of multi-colored papers with the other.

"Say, I'm glad I caught you, Blake," Horrie continued

25

with great good humor. "I was rooting around in my desk and found that I'd put the results of those time and motion studies in there instead of taking them home. We can go over them tonight if you'd like."

"But I can't . . ." protested Josh Blake again in desperation.

"Let's listen to this record first," Forcada said decisively. He twisted the volume control back to its original strength.

Jane tried, unsuccessfully, to keep a dignified expression on her face as she escaped through the door. She risked a tiny glance over her shoulder at Frederick Hall's new assistant.

As Josh Blake's eyes met hers, the tall lawyer looked very much like a man floundering in deep water who has just seen the one remaining life preserver float beyond reach.

# Chapter Two

∾ ∾ ∾

That appalled look of Josh Blake's came back to haunt Jane several times during the week that followed. It had just come to her mind again one sultry afternoon as she was finishing the day's work at her desk. She was annoyed that her memory of the incident hadn't dimmed appreciably in the interval, as it should have. Better still, she thought rebelliously, why couldn't she erase the entire episode from her mind? Why, indeed!

"Well, *rojita*—how did your day go?" asked the short man who stopped beside her desk.

"Maestro!" She jumped in surprise and came back to reality in a hurry. "I didn't see you!"

"Sorry, I didn't mean to startle you." The stocky, balding man peered at her over the top of his glasses. "It's a good thing that I have the high blood pressure instead of you. Otherwise . . ." His thumb shot toward the ceiling.

"I should stop daydreaming and pay attention," Jane

confessed with a crooked smile. "How *is* your blood pressure, by the way?"

"*Bien, bien.* I take the pills Dr. Jamieson gave me," the Spanish announcer assured her. He patted a bulging vest pocket. "Did you know that Emilio has scheduled an extra symphony performance on Thursdays?"

"Maestro, how wonderful!"

Her enthusiasm made the short man swell with pride. "I wanted to invite you into the control room during the broadcast, but you weren't around. After all, what's the use of being music director of the division if I can't—how do you say it? Like those things for muscle building . . ."

"Exercises?"

"*Sí. Eso es.* If I can't exercise my privileges—no?" He was carefully fitting a cigarette into a long amber holder as he spoke. "Anyhow, I missed you," he assured her.

"*Gracias,* Maestro."

"*De nada.*" He waved an airy hand and started down the hall. "I will check with you later and see if it's convenient for you to attend this week."

"I'll look forward to it," she promised. "Don't forget to take your pills."

As the maestro left, Horrie Cole came along and collapsed dramatically on the leather couch which was left over from the closing of the dispensary section. "Ah, *rojita—minha aureahsima.* I've missed you," he said.

"Horrie, you know that couch is supposed to be for staff personnel who aren't feeling well," she said mildly.

"Spare me." He put his hand over his heart theatrically. "You see before you a man tottering on the brink of exhaustion. After all, you haven't been around having your brains picked by Josh Blake all week."

"He's been making himself felt, then?" she asked with careful unconcern.

"That's an understatement." Cole stretched out at full length and pulled a pillow under his head. "He's delved into more things than a congressional investigating committee, and the hours he puts in—man oh man! Last night was the first night for him to leave with the carriage trade."

"Meaning what?"

"Look, why don't you stop fiddling with those schedules. You'll wear out the numbers in the shuffle," he complained. "Where was I? Oh, yes, the reason for Mr. Blake's abrupt departure at five o'clock. A blonde, *cara mia,* and what a blonde! Madge tells me it was Miss Barton."

"Miss Barton?"

"The daughter of J. C. Barton, vice-president in charge of sales at this dear old network. I will say for Josh Blake that he knows how to get ahead in the world. With a dish like that you could relax and enjoy job security. If I weren't married . . ."

". . . with a wife who is expecting a baby this month," Jane put in.

Horrie cocked an eyebrow at her. "Why the cold and stony? If my wife isn't unhappy about it, I can't see why you are." His round face broke into a mischievous grin. "Unless you've been nursing a secret passion for me all these weeks."

Jane broke into laughter. "That must be it."

Tom Carmichael appeared suddenly from around the corner. "This looks like a cozy get-together."

"It is," Cole said, moving reluctantly. "If you insist, I can share the couch."

"No, thanks." The traffic man gave the leather couch a derisive glance. "That thing still smells like a hospital—I don't know why they didn't throw it out. Besides, I just came to ask Jane if she wanted to gather with the clan across the street in a little while."

"Sorry, Tomás," she replied, shaking her head. "I have to do some errands on the way home tonight. May I take a rain check?"

"Sure." He shrugged. "But that puts the finishing touch to a thoroughly lousy day."

"I'm sorry."

"Never mind, Janie. I'm just in a stinking mood. I hoped it might improve in your company."

"That marketing course again? Or is that seventeenth-century literature giving you trouble?"

"Both. Plus some other things. I guess it's par for the course."

She wrinkled her nose at his pun. "But it would be nice if you could skip a few hazards."

"Hear, hear," applauded Cole. "Our homespun philosophy for the day."

"Watch it, Horrie, or I'll assign that beginning Portuguese announcer for your early show," she threatened.

Tom summoned a tired smile. "Do that, Janie. Well, I'm on my way. Hang onto your raincheck until, huh?"

"I'll do my best, Tom," she said gently.

"Wonder what's eating him?" Cole asked, watching the traffic manager stride back toward his desk.

"He's probably studying too hard. Getting a master's degree can be difficult, I imagine."

"You sound like an anxious mother hen," Cole said. "Young Tomás will survive. Besides, right now I need your help."

"Doing what?" Her tone was suspicious.

"Now look, *rojita*," he cajoled. "I've just had a marvelous idea. There's no reason why I couldn't put together a wonderful line graph one of these days when my wife starts having labor pains."

"You can't mean it!"

"I do, indeed. It might be very interesting if one approached that period scientifically and tried to time those pains accurately. No one can do a better timing job than I can. You can't tell what kind of important scientific data I might gather. Even the American Medical Association might be interested."

"You could submit it for a story idea to the program department first," she murmured.

"Very funny." Cole settled himself even more comfortably on the couch and pulled a stopwatch from one pocket and a scratch pad from another. "I thought we might try a sort of dry run or dress rehearsal."

"You'd better explain that comment."

"You know. I could get in some practice with you," he said impatiently.

"I'm scarcely in the same position as your wife," she pointed out, trying to swallow a smile.

"So you use your imagination." He pulled an automatic pencil from his shirt pocket. "Now I'm ready. If you can't throw yourself into that plot, just pretend you have acute indigestion—I don't care. All this fuss merely indicates the difference between the creative mind and the unimaginative one."

"It's a good thing we're not nearer Bellevue," she assured him, "or they might roll you off that padded couch and put you and your creative mind in a padded room."

His voice rose in exasperation. "Will you cooperate or won't you?"

"Very well. You don't mind if I check a supply inventory at the same time, do you?"

"Check away. You can start anytime. To make the experiment more valid, we might as well skip the earlier pains and begin when they're about two minutes apart."

She shot him a horrified look. "At the two-minute stage, I sincerely hope you'll be timing your wife's pains in the labor room of the hospital."

"Not unless I get in a decent rehearsal time."

"All right. I think you're barmy as a hoot owl, but I'll go along. If you're ready, I'll start with a short moan."

Fifteen minutes later, the inventory was checking beautifully and Horrie was still enthusiastically engrossed in his timing. He had only interrupted Jane once, telling her to "put some feeling in it." She had choked back a laugh and done her best. In fact, she was completing one of her finer efforts—a sigh that increased in volume before ending in a pathetic whimper—when a masculine voice said in concern, "For lord's sake, what's the matter?" The solicitude in Josh Blake's tone disappeared as he noticed Horrie stretched comfortably on the couch. "Okay, I give up. Clue me in, will you?"

The shock of his appearance made Horrie scramble for a more dignified position. At the same time, Jane's grasp on a sheaf of papers faltered and they slithered off her lap onto the floor.

"*Is* there something wrong?" Josh asked, his brows coming together in a sudden frown.

"Certainly not," she replied with dignity. "I was just having labor pains."

In the heavy silence that suddenly descended, she could almost see the ill-fated words in midair. As she raised a stricken hand to her lips, Horrie choked violently from his seat on the sidelines.

Josh Blake took a long time to survey her dispassionately—from head to toe—letting his glance linger at her trim twenty-four-inch waistline. "Those new miracle drugs certainly are amazing," he said finally. "Let me be the first to congratulate you."

He moved away toward his office, but not before Jane saw the corner of his stern mouth start to curve upward. Horrie was still rocking back and forth on the couch in silent glee when she rounded on him for lack of a more suitable victim.

"You can leave at any time," she informed him icily. "Your poor wife may have to put up with your inspirations, but from now on, cross me off the list."

"Okay, Janie." He was still laughing as he stood and came over to pat her shoulder consolingly. "Labor pains. Oh, *rojita,* you were wonderful! If you could have only seen your face afterward."

"Well, you certainly won't see it here any longer today," she said crossly. "I'm going to get my jacket and go home."

"I hope you're not going away mad."

"Not really," she admitted. "I'm just going, period. You'll have to find another straight man for the rest of your shift."

By the time she had draped her blue shantung blazer over her shoulders a few minutes later, her surge of irritation had disappeared. She peered in the mirror on the back of the closet door and straightened the collar of her ivory silk shirtwaist before brushing back a strand of hair from her forehead. She sighed gently, realizing there was no point in trying to look dignified if she encountered Josh Blake again. Not after her last faux pas. Hopefully, she'd escape without giving him a chance to utter any more sardonic comments.

Frederick Hall emerged from his office door just as she had retrieved her purse and was on her way out.

"How nice you look, my dear. Will you take pity on me

and join forces for a drink? Now, don't say no," he held up a hand as if to forestall her answer. "After all, you canceled our dinner engagement the other evening."

"Only because I had to work late," she assured him. "And tonight was the night I'd chosen to be efficient and get all my errands done.

"Nonsense." He looked at his watch. "You know the motto of the department 'Never do today . . .' "

". . . what you can put off 'til tomorrow." She smiled. "All right. You've talked me into procrastinating this time for the pleasure of your company. Shall we go?"

"I'll just see if Josh is ready—oh, here he is. Right on the dot." He greeted Blake, who was closing the door to his office behind him. "I've persuaded Jane to join us."

"I see," said Josh Blake, and then fell abruptly silent.

He needn't look as if he'd just come into contact with a smallpox carrier, she thought resentfully.

"Shall we go," said Frederick Hall, happily oblivious to all the byplay.

"By all means." Blake's slight bow toward Jane was ironic. "Our little mother in the middle."

"What's that?" Hall wanted to know.

"A private joke," Jane said, hurriedly moving up beside the older man and getting as far away from Joshua Blake as possible.

Madge hurried around the corner of the hallway just then. "Mr. Hall . . ."

The three of them pulled up and turned back to face her.

"I'm glad I caught you. That call you placed to Mexico City will be coming through any time now. The operator asked if you were ready to receive it."

"Blast!" murmured Hall, looking at his watch.

"It's all right," Jane cut in hurriedly. "We can get together another time."

"No, I won't hear of it." The International head motioned for Blake to take his place by Jane. "Josh can fill in for me. With any luck, that call should be through shortly and I'll be free to join you."

"Fine." Blake took Jane's elbow firmly and urged her on down the hall. "We'll see you over there, then."

"You don't have to be quite so officious." Jane shook off his clasp on her arm as they reached the end of the hallway.

"It's just that I prefer to fight in private. I think Fred Hall has enough problems right now without adding any more."

"You certainly should know," she told him unkindly.

They maintained a dignified silence across the street and into the corner restaurant. The shadowy recesses of the eating place after the bright sunshine outside made Jane hesitate and blink just inside the door.

Josh spoke up. "There seems to be an empty booth back there in the corner. Will that be all right?"

"Of course." This time, she gratefully accepted his guiding touch on her arm as they wended their way through the chattering customers clustered around small tables and standing at the long bar edging the big room.

At the empty booth, she sank into the soft, black leather seat and put her purse beside her. "Whenever I come in that door, I feel as if I need a seeing-eye dog for the first few minutes."

He settled onto the opposite bench. "I'd bet that the seeing-eye dogs will be needed more when that mob at the bar leaves. Do all those people belong to the network?"

"I'm the wrong person to ask," she told him, trying to

see through the smoky atmosphere. "I haven't been around the company long enough to recognize many people outside of our department. That's Tom Carmichael down at the end." She responded to the traffic manager's wave with a smile. "Now I'll have some explaining to do the next time I see him."

"You mean that your relationship entitles him to explanations?" Josh asked, his eyes narrowing thoughtfully.

"Certainly not."

"Then what *do* you mean?"

"I told Tom earlier that I didn't have time to stop in here today. Now I appear with you . . ."

"And he'll never believe how it all came to pass." There was sarcasm in Blake's voice. "Never mind, I'll furnish testimonials if you need them."

"You needn't be so unpleasant. It's just that I should have suggested another place when Uncle Fred—I mean, Mr. Hall—started all this."

Blake let that pass. "You can explain to Carmichael later," he told her coolly. "Besides, he seems to be well surrounded with friends. I can recognize half the Portuguese section, two of the French announcers, and at least one Spanish announcer."

"We could invite him to join us," she suggested.

"I think not; we have things to discuss." He offered her a cigarette which she refused and then put the pack on the table between them. "Is this a favorite stopping-off place?"

"I suppose you could say so." She didn't know whether to be annoyed or amused at his abrupt change of subject. "Perhaps it's because it's so dim that you can't see your superiors in here, or maybe it's just that people like to watch the tropical fish." She gestured toward the tanks of colorful fish set into the paneled walls around the room.

"At any rate, it's usually jammed. If people are on duty, they take their coffee breaks here. After working hours, it's generally something a little stronger."

He saw a harried waitress approaching. "This seems to be neatly timed. I think you're entitled to something a little stronger at this time of day. What will you have?"

"A Tom Collins please."

"One Tom Collins and a gin and tonic." He watched the girl wend her way back toward the bar and spoke absently. "It's just as well we have a breathing spell before Fred joins us. By the way, did he say that there wasn't a family relationship between you two?"

A flush spread over her cheeks. "That's right. When I was growing up, he was a close friend of my father's. We were in South America at the time, so he became *Tío Frederico*. Once in a while, I forget and the old name slips out."

He accepted her explanation with a casual nod. "I thought it was something like that. Incidentally, that chip you're carrying on your shoulder on his behalf isn't necessary." He ignored her annoyed gasp as he went on. "I also don't care for the role of Scrooge that you've allotted me in this affair. We'd better reach an understanding before you have half the department sticking pins in my effigy. That's why I wanted to talk to you alone."

"Correct me if I'm wrong. That sounds strangely like an ultimatum." Her voice was as devoid of emotion as his.

"It is. If you can't see your way toward cooperating, I'm afraid we'll have to dispense with your services." He lit his cigarette with unusual care and then stared levelly at her.

"I see." It was an effort to keep her tone bland, but she managed. "Do you realize that Mr. Hall is my superior and responsible for the employment of all International personnel?"

"I'm aware of that. If it were necessary"—his voice took on an edge—"and I sincerely hope it isn't—I think I could bring some influence to bear."

"Of course, I should have remembered." Her tone was suspiciously sweet. "You do have a special envoy of intercession with a vice-president. Mr. Barton, isn't it?"

"No, damn it. It isn't." A wave of red swept under his cheekbones.

Jane felt a surge of triumph at the crack in his composure and went on quickly, saying, "I also heard that you and Dr. Jamieson went to college together, but he doesn't have any influence on administrative policy. You can't count on him for help."

"Take my word for it, if you don't stop looking down your beautiful little nose at me, you'll be coordinating short wave transmissions at the Arctic Circle—" He broke off as the waitress arrived with their drinks. "The Tom Collins is for the lady," Josh advised her calmly, as if he and Jane had merely been holding forth on the summer weather.

As he reached for his wallet, Jane defiantly opened her purse and fumbled for her billfold. She'd choke before she'd let such an objectionable, opinionated oaf buy her anything.

"I'll pay," she announced doggedly before he could reach the check.

Josh shot her an annoyed glance which changed immediately into one of sheer deviltry. Deliberately he shoved his wallet back in his pocket. "It looks as if I've been outfumbled," he told the waitress solemnly. "The lady insists on paying."

Outraged but effectively silenced by his words, Jane

watched as the girl deducted the price of both drinks from the bill she'd offered.

Josh picked up his glass after the waitress left. "Very thoughtful of you," he said.

"I hope you choke on it!" The temper Jane had tried to contain boiled threateningly around the edges.

His smile was bland. "That's a different toast anyway." He took a thoughtful sip of his drink. "If it's any consolation, I felt like breaking your wrist when you reached for your wallet. Now, could we forget the last three minutes of our conversation while you listen to my side of the story? Please, Miss Chapin?" He watched the anger slowly fade from her eyes and a solemn little smile flit across her face.

"That 'please' was a master stroke of diplomacy," she said finally, picking up her glass.

"I'll bet you could even find a more appropriate toast if you worked on it." He was watching her intently now.

"Possibly. How about '*Salud y pesetas y tiempo para gozarles*'?" she asked. "*Y trataré de no derramar nada más sobre su traje.*"

"I'll need a translation."

"Health and wealth and time to enjoy them," she quoted easily, "and I'll do my best not to spill anything else on your suit."

His sober expression disappeared and he leaned back. "I should have known better than to ask." The amused look changed to one of appraisal. "Seriously, I think you have the wrong idea of my temporary appearance in International."

"I hope so."

"The powers that be have nothing against Fred Hall. They just thought he could use a few reserves."

She took a small sip of her drink and looked at him

over the top of the frosted glass. "And that means you?"

"That means me," he agreed. "But just temporarily. I doubt if you've paid much attention to congressional investigations lately, but some of our politicians are saying that Continental's venture into international broadcasting could be handled more efficiently by additional governmental transmission. They feel, and the reports up to now bear them out, that they're getting more per taxpayer dollar from their Washington transmissions than from this supplemental New York coverage that Continental is furnishing." He leaned forward to snub out his cigarette in the ashtray. "Naturally Continental takes a dim view of losing its international department or even of cutting it back. Right now, we're working on an accelerated policy to provide better coverage for the Latin American and South American fronts than the government can offer. That way, when congressional budget appropriation time rolls around, the network can be sure of getting its share. With unrest in the Caribbean and in Central America, it's especially important that the International Division do a proper job. Once we get the schedules and listener response beefed up, you'll be rid of me, and Fred Hall will be in full charge again."

"I see." Her voice became hesitant and suddenly shy. "How does one go about framing an apology to satisfy a Washington lawyer?"

"One forgets it," Josh said definitely. "I'm just glad we can be on the same side for a change. Up 'til now, I've felt as if I were in a private revolution and going down to defeat before I could dig a foxhole."

"I'm sorry," she said, her cheeks reddening slightly. To cover the awkward moment, she went on to ask, "What happens to you when you escape International's clutches? Or am I trespassing again?"

"Not a bit—I just wish I knew." His slow smile took years from his face. "Incidentally, you should never have considered me a threat in this department. Aside from some college Latin and French, I'm a linguistic numb-skull."

"It's hard to get it all from books," she assured him. "I tried once with some college Russian and I scarcely passed the 'hello,' 'how are you,' 'I love you,' and 'good-bye' stage in three months."

"At least, that vocabulary would get you further than 'The pen of my aunt is red,' or 'Which way to the Wagon-Lits office?' " he told her solemnly.

"I'll never know. After that course, it seemed safer to avoid all Russians."

"I see what you mean. By the way, I've been meaning to ask—why do they call you *'rojita linda'*?"

"They're just implying that there's a touch of red in my hair."

"And *linda* means pretty." He nodded. "Trust the South Americans to get it right."

"Well, they have me pegged right as far as redheaded temperament goes." She smiled mischievously. "You can testify to that."

"No way. That's called leading the witness."

"Okay, let's go back to a safer topic. What did you mean by saying you wished you knew what was going to happen in your future?"

He shrugged. "Just that. After this International stint, I can go back to my job in Continental's legal department in Washington or take up an offer to go into private practice here in New York."

The thought suddenly occurred to Jane that the elegant Miss Barton might be behind the New York proposition.

Josh went on as she remained discreetly silent. "I've

also had a tender from the Foreign Service section. That would mean an assignment to one of the smaller U.S. embassies in the beginning."

"Which do you want to do?"

"It isn't that simple. There are always responsibilities to consider as well as preferences." He grinned abruptly then. "I refuse to get stuck in a philosophical discussion so early in our acquaintance. Besides, in that outfit, you make it impossible for a man to keep his mind on the subject. You'd better have another drink and we'll discuss your future."

"No, thanks." She looked at her watch. "Since Uncle Fred apparently isn't going to make it, I'd better be going."

"A neat diplomatic withdrawal." He looked and sounded amused.

"Isn't it about time? After subjecting you to all my feline instincts."

"There *was* a small resemblance to a spitting kitten at one point," Josh agreed. "One of the marmalade variety."

"That's putting it too nicely. The truth is, I acted like a fully grown cat. Pure and simple."

"Since it's past tense, I refuse to argue," Josh said, grinning as he stood and watched her collect her purse. "However, I still plan to watch my step with you. Even marmalade kittens have to be reminded to sheathe their claws and purr at the proper intervals."

Jane thought that over as they left the restaurant and hesitated outside on the curb. "I'm not sure whether that's a compliment or not. Thank you for the . . ." She caught herself and substituted "for your company" smoothly.

This time his chuckle was deep. "And thank *you* for the drink. Are you going back up to the office?"

"Yes, I think I'd better tell Uncle Fred that I have to get on home."

He watched the traffic light change and guided her across the street. "I'll come along with you. There are some papers I meant to get from my office and a message I wanted to leave with Forcada. Do you suppose he's still around?"

"Probably, if Anita's on shift."

They climbed the one flight of stairs to International's back entrance more companionably this time, side by side.

"Surely you know why he's putting in all the extra time," Jane went on as Josh pulled open a door for her.

"No. Should I?"

"Well, I suppose it might help your cause if you're counting on great efficiency from his section," she said slowly. "Otherwise, I'd have to admit that it's plain gossip."

They went on through the main door of the department and surveyed the long room. At the far end, Frederick Hall's office door stood wide open, showing a deserted interior.

"Uncle Fred must be around somewhere," Jane said, glancing again at her watch. "Maybe he's in the music library talking to Emilio."

"Let's go see." Josh guided her toward the hallway. "I wish you'd get on with the rest of your story."

"There's really not much to tell. Just that Emilio Forcada and Anita are a devoted twosome these days," she said as they rounded the corner to the music library.

"What's so damned fascinating about that? I suppose sooner or later they'll resolve the issue. Maybe even get engaged. They're certainly old enough to do what they please."

She glanced up at him and shook her head. "There you go again," she complained. "Who's leaping off on a tangent this time? The only reason I brought the whole thing up is that Emilio and Anita can't get engaged for the simple reason that he's already married."

Blake gave a soundless whistle of surprise.

"And his estranged wife happens to be the daughter of the dictator on one of those hot little Caribbean islands our government is trying to cajole for a U.S. missile base." They had stopped in the doorway of the music library by this time and Jane spoke in lowered tones. She looked somewhat guiltily over her shoulder before she continued. "It looks deserted back there, but I'd hate to have Anita hear me."

He nodded reflectively. "So she and Forcada seem determined to go ahead and get married?"

"That puts it nicely. Everyone is discreetly hoping to sidetrack the affair. *Tío*—I mean Uncle Fred has tried to point out the political repercussions as well as the religious ones for Emilio. If he applies for a Mexican divorce as they plan, his wife will probably raise a furor and the publicity will be dreadful. Now that you've mentioned International's position concerning the congressional appropriation, it's worse than ever."

"You're damn right." There was cold anger in his voice. "Could you tell me why it has taken me a week to find this out?"

"I suppose because Uncle Fred was hoping he could talk Emilio out of it in time and no one else would discuss it with you," she said defensively. "Besides, what could you have done?"

"I'm not sure." Josh's look was decidedly thoughtful. "I told you that responsibilities mean a lot to me. I mean to have this assignment go off right."

Jane's eyebrows climbed. "Even if you did all your homework, I don't see what difference it would make. Emilio and Anita wouldn't be swayed by editorial comments, would they?"

"I don't know yet." His stern expression twisted slightly, as if he found her remark amusing but not as if he were particularly amused. "After all, Anita is a woman. There are ways to accomplish most anything." He flushed as he saw the color drain from her face. "We were talking about possibilities," he added in a suddenly harsh tone, "not necessarily probabilities."

"I see." She looked at him steadily. "You must forgive my naïveté. Perhaps I've been out of the country too long. There's a proverb I could mention."

"And what's that, Maid Marian?" he asked with sarcasm.

"Never muddy the water; you may have to drink it."

There was leashed fury in his movement toward the nearest timing room door. "Let's get on with our search," he grated out. "I have an appointment later on."

"Certainly," Jane replied just as tersely. Joshua Blake could have all the appointments he wanted—blonde ones like Miss Barton or sultry brunettes like Anita Warren. They'd probably be standing in line for him to make a choice.

That thought brought about a pain that was almost physical, and Jane grimaced with annoyance as she reached for another timing room door. "This is just a waste of time," she said. "Probably Emilio has gone and Uncle Fred had a change of plans . . ." Her voice trailed off when Josh's suddenly arrested movement nearby claimed her attention. He stood motionless at the threshold of the third timing room, his hand white with strain as he clutched the edge of the door. Then, jerkily, like a character in slow motion, he moved again. This time, he disappeared into the room. Wordlessly, she threw herself after him.

Crumpled silently at his feet lay the long-limbed figure of the Spanish department head.

Emilio Forcada had one arm twisted under him. The other pointed like an accusing symbol toward the slowly revolving turntable above him. The needle arm was tracing a monotonous circle at the center of the acetate disc and making a sibilant moaning sound in the process. Jane suddenly realized it was the only sound in the room.

Abruptly her first-aid training asserted itself and she crouched beside the pathetic figure, fingers fumbling for a pulse.

"My god," Josh said in a hushed voice, "he's still got a stopwatch clutched in his hand."

Jane was intent on counting the thready pulse. "It's strange he didn't drop it when he felt the attack coming on."

Josh's glance had moved to the bloody area almost hidden at the back of Forcada's head. "There was no warning for this. I think someone tried to kill him."

"The only important thing now is that he needs help. Go to the office and call Dr. Jamieson," Jane said. "Then phone for an ambulance. I'll have to get some blankets from that closet by my desk."

"Stay here! I'll be back with them as soon as I can." Josh was gone in an instant.

Jane remained huddled beside Emilio Forcada's barely breathing body. She felt almost desperately for his pulse again. The big South American was failing perceptibly.

Unless Dr. Jamieson arrived soon, International's most pressing political problem would have resolved itself.

# Chapter Three

≈ ≈ ≈

From that point on, events occurred almost too rapidly for Jane to comprehend.

Josh was quickly back with blankets under his arm and then gone again.

He was followed in short order by Mark Jamieson, who gave Jane's ministrations an approving glance before he knelt beside her and the unconscious Forcada. "Good girl," he said, opening his black bag, "better check with Josh to see if that ambulance is on its way. I'll take over here."

She nodded gratefully, getting to her feet and hurrying to the outer hall, where she discovered a security guard planted in the main doorway.

"I've got my orders," he was saying to the group of irate individuals in front of him. "Mr. Blake said nobody was to go in, and that's the way it's going to be."

"But I have a program in ten minutes," Maestro Betancourt was protesting. "I must get my script and stopwatch from the timing room. Don't you understand, I can't waste time out here."

"And I need some records," a Portuguese announcer put in. "Anita said she'd have them ready. How am I supposed to broadcast a show without them?"

Just then, Josh Blake arrived back on the scene, his tall figure flanked by two prowler-car policemen. "It's all right, officer," he told the security guard. "I can sort this out." Turning to Jane, he asked, "Is Mark still with Forcada?"

She nodded. "Dr. Jamieson sent me out to check on the ambulance."

"It's on the way. Stick around," he ordered, before motioning the policemen on into the library and turning to the International staff. "Maestro, you'd better get an extra stopwatch and script from the production section. Silva, I'd suggest that you pick up some standby records from the cabinet in your section. The rest of you," he said firmly, "had better get back to your desks."

Jane noted with surprise that the group dispersed without protest, apparently glad to have someone take charge.

Josh lingered by her side long enough to ask in a low voice, "How's Forcada doing?"

"Holding his own—just barely. I'd better get back."

He nodded. "I'll send the ambulance attendants in the moment they arrive."

Jane hurried back to the by now crowded timing room. "Any minute for the ambulance," she assured the doctor.

"Good." He glanced up at the two policemen who were watching quietly from the corner. "He seems to be maintaining a satisfactory level for the moment, but I'll feel better when we get him to the hospital."

The older officer nodded. "I'd say that your Mr. Forcada is lucky not to be on a homicide report right now."

A depressing silence settled on the room. Jane knelt to tuck the blanket more firmly around the unconscious man's feet, noting that the turntable had been stopped while she was gone but that the yellow pages of Emilio's script were still scattered about the floor. The stopwatch had apparently slipped from his grasp and lay on the linoleum next to his outflung hand. Strange that he should have taken the maestro's watch, she thought—or was it? After all, an announcer might borrow a stopwatch the way anyone else would pick up a pencil from a desktop. Horrie Cole could confirm that.

Aloud, she asked, "Shall I straighten things up in here?" She indicated the scattered sheets of script with a nod of her head.

"Never mind, miss. We'll leave it 'til the lieutenant comes," the younger officer said.

At that point, two ambulance men came bustling in bearing a lightweight metal stretcher. They were accompanied by a competent-looking young man carrying a medical bag. His keen eyes took in Dr. Jamieson's obvious control of the situation.

"Looks as if I could have saved myself a trip," he said good-naturedly.

Jamieson nodded and introduced himself. "Do you think there's room for me in the ambulance?" he asked. "I'd like to have a word with your neurosurgery people before I relinquish the case."

"You bet, sir," the intern said eagerly. "Glad to have you along. I'll follow the stretcher down."

"Be right with you then." Jamieson paused in the hallway. "I'll be in touch," he told the policemen. He turned to Jane, saying in an undertone, "Tell Josh I'll call him later, either here or at home." He gave her arm a friendly pat and hurried 'round the corner.

He had scarcely left when a middle-aged man wearing a rumpled gray suit strolled into the timing room. There was another policeman with him, wearing a meticulously pressed uniform, but it was the older man who nodded to the two officers in the corner of the room and said, "Let's hear what you've got, boys. Right after I talk to this young lady." He let his calm glance linger on Jane. "You must be Miss Chapin," he announced.

His matter-of-fact manner put her immediately at ease. "That's right," she replied. "I was looking after Señor Forcada until the ambulance arrived."

"So Mr. Blake said." His deep tone became confidential and apologetic. "I'm Lieutenant Nolan. I'd like a few words with you, but I'd better catch up with my homework first."

"I understand," she said. "Would you like me to wait outside?"

"If you wouldn't mind. I won't be long."

Jane nodded and slipped past the heavy door out into the music library. As she walked behind the counter to perch on a table, her thoughts were concerned with the wounded Emilio—wondering whether he would rally as Mark Jamieson hoped. Certainly the announcer's strength and rugged physique should help in his recovery.

Then she frowned as another thought occurred to her. Where was Anita Warren when it all happened? Usually the music librarian and Emilio spent most of their working hours together. And—if rumor was to be believed— their leisure time as well. Jane surveyed the girl's vacant desk, deciding that her schedule might have been changed for some reason. Tom Carmichael would probably know about that, since all department schedules came automatically under traffic desk supervision.

Jane looked thoughtful as her imagination moved on. Tom was probably busy assisting Josh Blake, trying to calm the chaos in the Spanish section. Or maybe Mr. Blake needed more than mortal help. It might take divine intervention to smooth over a case of assault and battery for the New York police. Or for a congressional committee. Especially for the politicians—if the broadcast appropriation emerged unscathed.

It was like a soap opera teaser at the end of the program, Jane thought with some irony. Would Emilio recover to tell who attacked him? Would Anita be able to shed any light on the tragedy? Was there a political motivation behind the whole affair? Tune in tomorrow and learn the answers.

She shivered then as a surge of nausea suddenly swept over her. Her initial reaction was to close her eyes, but found that she had to cling to the table for support. "Oh heavens, not now," she murmured to herself and swallowed hard. "Lieutenant Nolan had better hurry."

As if in answer to her whispered request, the door to the timing room opened abruptly and the three uniformed policemen emerged and disappeared down the hallway toward the studios. Lieutenant Nolan stood in the doorway for a moment staring thoughtfully after them, and then turned and beckoned to Jane. "Sorry to have made you wait, young lady. Would you come back in and fill some of the blank spaces for me?"

"Of course, Lieutenant." Jane took a steadying breath and decided that her nausea had passed for the moment. Maybe she'd make it yet!

. She walked back to the timing room and paused for an instant, staring curiously around the newly straightened premises. The stopwatch was resting atop the quiet turntable; the acetates were stacked neatly next to it. The paper cloud of script had been put in a semblance of order beside them. The dark stain on the floor, however, was still in evidence.

"You don't look well, Miss Chapin." Nolan was peering at her sharply. "I thought people who worked in the media were used to violence."

"I don't think any person gets used to violence." She smiled wryly. "There were several revolutions in South America when I was growing up, but I still jump when a gun goes off."

He looked slightly disconcerted. "That makes sense, I guess. If this has upset you, maybe we'd better postpone the rehash."

"You've got your facts mixed in my case," she replied, swallowing again with an effort. "I really feel as bad as I look. It's not poor Emilio, though, but a virus inoculation which is just catching up with me."

"Would you rather wait and talk to me later?"

She shook her head. "I don't think so. If this follows the course that Dr. Jamieson anticipates, I'll be down for forty-eight hours. Let me tell you what I saw and then take a cab home." She waited for his approving nod before launching into a concise synopsis of what she and Josh Blake had found when they came upon Forcada's crumpled figure.

Lieutenant Nolan heard her story out before asking, "Is this place as easy to get into as it seems?"

"I'm afraid so. There are entrances both from the domestic and the international departments. During the busy hours, there is usually so much activity that people line up for help from the music librarians. However, at the slack times of day, when the announcers have all their shows covered and the producers are ready, there's no need to maintain too much staff."

Nolan shook his head in bewilderment. "You've lost me along the way."

"Not really," she said, patiently resisting an urge to lay her throbbing head against the cool plastered wall. "It's just broadcast jargon. Mr. Hall, who's head of International or Tom Carmichael, the traffic manager, will be able to explain it much more concisely."

"What about Mr. Blake?"

"Mr. Blake certainly," she said with emphasis. "It's just that he's new to our division and I'm not used to thinking of him in connection with International operations. Was there anything else you wanted with me?"

"Maybe you could take a look at this stuff and see if there's anything out of the way."

She walked hesitantly over to the record turntable. "I'm really not the one you should be asking. Departmental coordination is more in my line."

"I'll take a chance." His deep voice swept her objections aside. "I gather a stopwatch is in general use here."

She nodded and indicated the one on the table. "That one belongs to Maestro Betancourt."

" 'Maestro'?"

"That's because he handles all the classical music programs for the section. He told me a few minutes ago that Emilio—Mr. Forcada—had borrowed his watch earlier."

"So it wasn't unusual?"

"I don't think so. Most of the people in the department have their own stopwatches." She shrugged. "I suppose Emilio had mislaid his."

"That's what I thought you'd say," Nolan commented. "How about the records?"

He watched as she gingerly held the edges of the big acetates and read the titles.

"You'd probably get a better answer from the maestro, but they look fine to me. Mainly rhumbas and tangos. I guess Emilio was picking out some background music. He was thinking of putting together a poetry show to be scheduled once a week, and this was a pilot show. Mr. Blake or Tom Carmichael could tell you about that. Was there anything else you wanted to ask?"

"Just take a look at this pile of script," he said, "and afterward I'll send you home in a police car."

"If you don't mind, I'll stick with a cab. Otherwise, the superintendent at my apartment building would never let me forget it." She was scanning the pile of typewritten pages as she spoke and finally looked up to say hesitantly, "This looks all right. Of course, it's part Spanish and part English, but Emilio was completely bilingual so that wouldn't matter to him."

"You think he wrote it himself?"

"Normally not." She continued to leaf through the pages. "They have special staff for scriptwriting. But since this was a pilot show and a special project of Señor Forcada's, he might have been doing the writing as well. Probably he was choosing his own musical selections and doing the reference work on the poetry . . ." Her voice trailed off.

"What's the matter?"

"Oh, I'm sorry." She rubbed her forehead wearily with the back of her hand. "I was just thinking this page didn't sound like Emilio."

"Let me see."

Heads together, they scanned the lines of typing on the yellow paper.

Send home my harmless heart againe,
Which no unworthy thought could staine;
But if it be taught by thine
To make jestings
Of protestings
⠀⠀And crosse both
⠀⠀Word and oath,
Keepe it, for then 'tis none of mine.

Nolan rubbed his thumb raspingly over his rugged chin. "It beats me. Sure isn't the kind of stuff for light listening."

"Just what I was thinking." Jane took a sudden indrawn breath and shook her head as if to clear it. "I'd better leave now."

"Or I'll have another stretcher case on my hands, is that it?" He put a helpful hand under her elbow and walked with her to the door.

"Nothing so drastic," she assured him, trying to keep her teeth from chattering. "Let's just hope I can find a cab before we meet anyone else. The only company I pine for right now is a hot water bottle."

Unfortunately the gods weren't cooperating. Josh Blake and Dr. Mark Jamieson practically ran them down as they rounded the corner.

The young doctor beamed impartially on them. "How's that for a quick round trip? I was able to leave Forcada in the care of a neurologist I know at the hospital. Barring complications, he thinks things look pretty good."

Josh observed Nolan's supporting hand at Jane's elbow and interrupted brusquely. "What's wrong with you?" he asked her.

"There's nothing really wrong," Jane replied in a tone that meant nothing of the kind. It was bad enough to feel rotten without meeting everybody she knew on the way to her sickbed. The only thing lacking was editorial comment. That, too, wasn't long in coming.

"You look terrible," Josh said in a decisive tone.

"Thanks very much. I wasn't thinking of entering a beauty contest at the moment."

He was obviously puzzled by the way she snapped at him. "There's no need to get upset," he replied. "I only meant that—"

"I *know* what you meant." She tried for a morsel of dignity. "Let's go, Lieutenant."

"Go where?" Jamieson and Blake chorused.

"The lady is going home," Nolan said.

"I remember," Jamieson snapped his fingers. "It's that virus injection you were bent on trying."

"Go to the head of the class, Doctor," she said, trying to smile. "I'm afraid you were right when you said I might not be sufficiently acclimated to avoid side effects."

"What were you thinking of, trying a fool thing like that?" Blake lashed out at them.

"It certainly was not a fool thing." Jamieson was on his professional dignity. "We were attempting to ascertain—"

"If you'll excuse me," Jane said in a weak voice, "I'll be getting along so you can tell Lieutenant Nolan more about Emilio's condition. The only thing I could add to any discussion is the very real probability that I'll get sick in the middle of it."

To the credit of both men, the discussion stopped abruptly.

"We'd better get you home." Josh took the other elbow.

"There's no need for you to leave." Jamieson moved in to intercept him. "I'll see her home myself."

Jane felt like a bone being fought over by two stubborn

and determined watchdogs. At any other time, her ego would have soared in response. Most presentable females are not averse to having two men rally 'round. At that particular moment, however, Jane would have traded both of them in for a quiet bed where she could rest her aching bones in peace.

Again the decision was taken from her. This time, by a statuesque female who would have raised the blood pressure of any man outside of a mummy case.

She was a gorgeous blonde wearing a grapefruit-colored silk sheath that was worth every dollar of the bank draft it must have cost.

Even in ordinary circumstances, the newcomer would have offered stiff competition. As it was, the shaded rings under Jane's eyes suffered in comparison with the emerald and diamond dinner ring on the other's right hand, and Jane's parchment color was quite different from the taller woman's translucent skin tones.

The blonde's voice was carefully modulated, but she couldn't hide an edge of irritation as she said, "Josh, darling, I've been waiting forever. What in the world kept you?"

"I'm sorry, Ellen. I should have called you. I don't think you've met these people. Miss Chapin, Lieutenant Nolan, Dr. Jamieson—this is Miss Barton."

For Jane, the introduction was the last, numbing blow. Her stomach churned in instant rebellion and her head throbbed with pain. She managed to murmur, "How do you do, Miss Barton," before she gave way and gasped, "Oh, lord, I'm going to be sick!"

There was only an instant for her to note that even statuesque blondes didn't look very good when they stared, open-mouthed, in horror. After that, Jane didn't linger. She turned and ran frantically for the nearest exit.

# Chapter Four

### ∾ ∾ ∾

Josh Blake recalled that exit as he stood waiting for the elevator in the tiny foyer of Jane's apartment house three days later. If he had been strictly honest with himself, he would have acknowledged that he had been thinking of her precipitous departure and her pale, unhappy face considerably more than was necessary in the interim.

It wasn't that he was left in the dark about her condition. Madge Waverly had been faithful in issuing daily reports on Jane's health. Horrie Cole had digressed at length about the message he'd penned to accompany the division's bouquet of flowers. Even Mark had spent a long lunch telling of Jane's insistence that she help him test his latest research venture.

Josh also knew there was no official need for him to call on Jane, and considering their brief and fiery acquaintance, it might even be awkward if he found her at home.

Thus, aware of his inconsistency but not wanting to explore it, he gave the elevator button another decisive push. When it finally arrived, he punched the indicator for the twelfth floor almost grimly.

There were just two doors in the tiny vestibule when he arrived. One was a startling Chinese red with a writhing, dragonlike creature in brass for a doorknob. Reluctantly, he went toward it. The brass plate over the bell proclaimed that a Madame Trimpani occupied the premises. Neatly thumbtacked above the plate was a calling card identifying Miss Jane Chapin.

An odd choice of roommates, he thought as he pushed the bell. Where in the devil did she pick up a Madame Trimpani? Sounded like a character from a low-budget Italian movie. He heard a masculine voice saying "I'll get it" on the other side of the Chinese red entrance, and then the door swung abruptly open to reveal the figure of Tom Carmichael.

"Well, Mr. Blake," the traffic manager said, "you're the last person I expected . . ." His voice trailed off as he realized that his comment wouldn't win him any popularity award.

"Is Miss Chapin here?" Blake's tone was curt.

"Sure, she'll be right out." Carmichael gestured vaguely behind him. "Come on in."

Josh followed him through the slate entranceway and paused as the blinding decor of the living room met his eyes. "Good God," he muttered. "I don't believe it."

"Pretty awful, huh?" Tom conceded amiably.

"Awful" was putting it mildly.

Pale yellow walls were the only restful area that could be seen in the entire room. Certainly the furnishings didn't qualify under that heading. A deep purple davenport bulged with down cushions and took up the better part of one side of the room. Elsewhere, there were spindly occasional chairs upholstered in a shiny red satin. Scatter rugs of purple and red shag covered polished hardwood floors, while gilt coffee and lamp tables with fragile legs were tucked in odd places. Above everything, a monstrous mobile featuring oddly shaped pieces of colored glass hung from the ceiling like a contemporary sword of Damocles.

There wasn't one serene spot in the entire room, Josh decided. And then his glance focused suddenly on the slight figure in a beige outfit standing in an archway across the room and he abruptly changed his mind.

Jane was dressed casually in trim-fitting slacks, a white turtleneck shirt, and a beige, v-necked sweater. Her face was devoid of makeup except for a pale application of lipstick. To Josh Blake's eyes, she looked as out of place in that garish room as a switchblade knife at a P.T.A. rummage sale.

If Jane's outward demeanor appeared tranquil, the aura was misleading. Josh had often thought of her abrupt departure three days before and smiled about it, but Jane's memories hadn't been so easy to handle. Very few women choose to look like a remnant on a clearance table in front of people like Mark Jamieson and Joshua Blake. Obviously Mark had seen far worse specimens in his career, but Josh . . .

At that point, her mind had given up trying to rationalize. And as for Ellen Barton, the recollection of her presence had set Jane's recovery back a good six hours. It was just pride, Jane reasoned, but hers was up in arms again as she saw Josh's figure across the room.

She settled her shoulders back more firmly. "Good afternoon, Mr. Blake. How nice of you to stop by." Too late, she realized that she sounded like some prim figure in a drawing room comedy.

If Josh noted the resemblance, he was smart enough to ignore it. "I'm glad to find you looking—er—feeling so much better," he said, not setting the world afire with *his* dialogue, either. "Everybody in the department sent their best."

"That's kind of them," Jane said, aware of how quickly he'd abandoned the subject of her appearance. If he felt she was such a sight, why in the dickens did he have to come and mention it?

Tom evidently didn't like the thick silence which neither of the participants chose to break. "Well, I'd better be on my way," he said finally. "I'm due across town in about fifteen minutes. This is my day for the split shift," he told Josh in explanation.

"Tom was kind enough to stop by after his classes," Jane said.

"I see." Blake's remark was noncommittal.

Carmichael didn't appear to notice. "I don't know whether I cheered Janie or whether it was the other way around. That Lit class I had this afternoon left me against the wall." He hesitated by the front door before opening it. "Hope we see you back tomorrow, Janie. Say good-bye to the chaperone for me. So long, Mr. Blake."

Josh's expression was unreadable as he watched the door close behind him. "I hope he didn't hurry away," he said, with a lack of conviction in his voice. His tone changed, however, as he stared at her and went on to say, "Maybe you've had too much company today. You still look awfully pale."

"I'm just fine. Mark tells me I can go back to work tomorrow. There's absolutely no reason—" She broke off as a large black and white cat with a bobbed tail stalked into the room. "Fig, where in the world were you hiding?"

Josh frowned more noticeably. "Fig?"

"That's for Figaro." For the first time since his arrival, Jane smiled. "Madame wasn't very original."

"I'm not with you."

"It's not complicated." She picked up the cat from where he was rubbing her ankles and walked over to the couch with him. "Fig is part of my sublet from Madame Trimpani along with the rest of the apartment. Madame's an opera coach when she's in town, but right now she's communing with nature in Maine."

"I see." Josh felt a strange relief. "Then all this"—his sweeping gesture included the room and its startling decor—"belongs to the Madame?"

"Every ghastly bit," she assured him solemnly. "She probably would have dyed Fig purple if he hadn't objected. I'm tempted to wear sun glasses in here even on a cloudy day."

"At least you have a nice view," he said, going to the window.

"It really is," Jane agreed. "All the way across Manhattan from in here, and from the bedroom and kitchen, there's a dandy view of the United Nations and the East River. Fortunately, the paint in the bedroom is a little more subdued or I'd have suffered a relapse," she added ruefully.

Josh's expression became more forbidding. "I don't know what Mark was thinking of—using you as a guinea pig for his theories."

"There wasn't any danger," she flared. "He's much too good a doctor to take chances like that. Besides, I insisted."

"I still say he should have known better."

"That's ridiculous!" She paid no attention as the cat slipped from her clasp and stalked toward Josh who was still by the window. "You have no right to set yourself up as judge and jury in my case, Mr. Blake."

"Don't start making generalizations, Miss Chapin"—his voice had a sarcastic edge—"merely because I question—ouch! What the hell . . ." He bent toward his ankle but halfway down found his hand suddenly attacked by needle-sharp teeth. "Dammit, let go of me, you menace, or I'll—"

Jane hurled herself toward the offender and pried his jaws from Josh's wrist. "Fig, cut it out! You terrible cat!"

The "terrible cat" leaped lightly out of her hands and jumped with unconcern to the top of the purple davenport. There he proceeded to wash a paw with no further interest in the two people by the window.

"I'm terribly sorry," Jane said. "Let me see your wrist. Oh gosh, it's bleeding on the cuff of your shirt. You'd better come and let me clean it up."

Much to his amazement, Josh found himself propelled into a white-tiled bathroom whose only departure from the conventional was a rack of purple towels. Before he could protest, Jane ran warm water over the back of his hand and soaped the scratches gently. Finally she blotted the skin and applied a cool antiseptic.

"Now, about your ankle," she began.

"It's fine," he assured her. "Just a nip that startled me." He finished drying his hands. "There was no need to fuss over this," his tone was brusque and embarrassed, "but thanks all the same."

Her smile was whimsical. "I feel somewhat responsible."

He followed her back into the living room. "Don't you feed the beast?"

"I'm afraid he's just part cannibal. Although from the looks of him"—she cast a critical gaze at the unconcerned Fig—"I really think he's just part cat. A friend came by one day and suggested I throw a saddle on him."

"I could make a suggestion too, but it wouldn't be that charitable. Maybe he shares your antipathy toward lawyers."

"Not at all," she said coolly. "There's just no accounting for his taste. Right now, he seems to regard you as an appetizer before dinner. Next time you come, he may be your bosom buddy. That is . . ."

"Assuming there is a next time," Josh finished for her. "At least, we have a case for discussion."

"I don't know what you're talking about."

He gave her a cynical look. "Any intelligent woman would know what I'm talking about. Whatever your other failings, you don't lack for gray matter."

She bit her lip and tried to keep from laughing. "I'm not sure whether I should say 'thank you' or challenge you to a duel." When he didn't reply, she glanced at him more closely and, for the first time, noticed lines of fatigue at the corners of his eyes. "Let's declare a truce for the afternoon. Could I offer you a drink?"

His slow smile appeared briefly. "You could—if you'll let me offer dinner later."

Jane felt a twinge and tried to hide her disappointment. "I'm sorry. Uncle Fred called earlier with a dinner invitation."

"Perhaps another time," Josh replied, unconcerned. "I'll accept that drink, though. If you have time."

"Of course. I'll let you be bartender in the kitchen." She led the way toward a pullman kitchen which was severely functional in green and white.

"Your landlady must have run out of purple paint." He was opening the cupboard door she indicated.

"Maybe she felt the kitchen was beneath her notice. Can you find what you want in there? My liquor stock is pretty limited."

"Scotch and soda will be fine," he said, pulling out the bottles. "What about you? Brandy's supposed to be medicinal if you need an excuse."

"I'll remember," she said solemnly. "In the meantime, a glass of sherry sounds better. I'll get some ice cubes out of the refrigerator for you." After Josh fixed his drink and handed her the glass of wine, she said, "Let's go back into the living room. The color scheme is awful, but the furniture isn't bad for comfort."

"Maybe the thing to do is sit down and drink with your eyes closed," he said.

She smiled and perched on the metal cover of a radiator in front of the windows.

"Now's the time for you to make polite noises about the weather," he drawled as he settled down and leaned his head against a convenient cushion.

"Should I?" She swirled the sherry in her glass absently. "All right, I'll play. What *is* the forecast?" At least, such inane conversation would give her a chance to show him that his presence didn't affect her, and after her last appearance, she certainly needed some brownie points.

"They said shower activity." Josh sounded as if he didn't have his mind on the subject either. "A fancy way of saying it'll rain like hell before midnight."

"It would be nice if they'd say so."

"Why be different? The politicians speak a different language, and so do the newspaper reporters." He took a sip of his drink. "I think doctors have avoided plain En-

65

glish for years. Mark told me they learn a special set of phrases right at the beginning."

"You mean—like cases being terminal instead of saying the patient died?"

"Sure. Or suffering loss of vision rather than going blind."

"Lawyers are just as guilty," she pointed out. "Or don't you admit that?"

He opened his eyes then and glanced mockingly at her. "Of course. Just like now. We're indulging in conversational drivel that's safe and dull. It reminds me of a TV movie I saw on grasshoppers—where they spent eight hours rubbing their feet together before getting around to important things."

"I think you mean crickets," Jane replied, without thinking. "And it was a mating dance."

"Very possibly. Let's skip the eight-hour preliminaries, shall we?"

Her eyes went wide. "I beg your pardon?"

A piratical grin flickered over his lean face. "I just meant we should get down to the nitty-gritty in our discussion. It wasn't a pitch for—anything else." There was a distinct hesitation before he tacked on the last two words.

Jane decided it would be safer to ignore that. Distinctly safer. "I'd like to hear what's been going on at work while I've been away," she said, trying to sound as if she meant it.

"In good time." Josh reached behind his head and adjusted a pillow more comfortably. "Right now, I'd like to find out more about you."

She almost choked on her sip of sherry. "For heaven's sake—why?"

"I don't know." He sounded genuinely puzzled. "To be

honest, I'm not often curious about what makes people tick."

Her slow smile betrayed an elfin quality. "I'm sure you're not. It's been apparent from the very first."

"You mean, my attempt at self-preservation?"

"Now who's hiding behind words?" she chided him. "It's the old 'live and let live' policy of the average man."

"That remark makes you sound about ninety years old," he commented, poking an ice cube in his drink and watching it surface again. "What's wrong with a 'hands off' policy?"

"Nothing in itself," she admitted. "Mostly it goes along with a strong tendency to become insular. Ever since I've been in New York, I've been frustrated by it. Do you know that a cab driver told me the other day that he'd never been out of this borough? Furthermore, he had no desire to ever go."

"I hope you arranged for him to visit the nearest psychiatrist."

"Hardly. I followed your 'hands off' policy," she mocked. "Seriously, it was the man's lack of curiosity that appalled me."

Josh's expression was hard to fathom. "That's a big soap box you're trying to crawl on. Watch out for splinters."

"I apologize." She saluted him with her wine glass. "People on soap boxes get very dull after the first five minutes."

"No, don't change the subject. You think I should have displayed more curiosity in the beginning. In what way?"

"I'm not sure." Her glance met his and held it. "You give the impression of complete control—both in your private life and in your career. Almost as if you'd make an appointment to cope with an emergency. You're suave, sophisticated, reeking with assurance, and somehow too pat."

"Dammit," he complained, "you make me sound like a TV commercial."

"I didn't mean to." She shook her head ruefully. "I apologize for my manners. Maybe I stayed in South America too long."

"Why don't you sit down here and stop fiddling with those curtains," he said, indicating the davenport cushion beside him. "Besides, you can't change the subject now. I'm fascinated by this character analysis. What evidence do you have for that 'hard and heartless' summation?"

She sat down on the couch but edged toward the arm so she could turn and face him. "Not hard," she denied. "Detached. I'll bet I can prove it. Do you have an apartment in Washington?"

He nodded, amused.

"How many other apartments on the floor?"

"About six," he admitted.

"Can you give me the name of two other tenants on the floor?"

"I can go you one better," he said, smiling wryly. "I can't even give you the name of one."

"That's what I mean."

"Good lord, girl—people who are busy don't have time to run back and forth with casseroles to welcome the new neighbors."

"Now you're making fun of me," she admonished. "And a casserole wasn't what I had in mind. A little simple kindness is possible even among busy people. But let it pass. I'm afraid you and I are wavelengths apart in the way we think."

"I shouldn't wonder." The reserve was back in his

tone. "Did you find time to satisfy your curiosity in South America?"

"Heavens, no. I just whetted it some more. Working abroad is always fascinating, though. It's important not to lose your sense of humor—no matter what happens. I'll have to admit mine was stretched to the limit a time or two."

"From what I hear, that's par for the course," Josh said idly. "Where do you go after this stint with International?"

"Out to the Northwest, where my family lives on a small ranch in the mountains. Before my father retired, we just spent our holidays and vacations there. I've been promised air that hasn't been recycled and a fresh crop of saddle horses and burros."

"Sounds great. Then what?"

"I sign another contract with my favorite oil company—only I'll work in the Middle East this time. They're generous with travel time, so I plan to spend a few days in London en route, then work my way through Italy and revisit Istanbul."

"Why Istanbul?"

"Why not?" she countered. "It's a beautiful spot. Some friends are stationed there, and we'll go boating on the Bosphorus, sightsee in the Blue Mosque, and eat kebab in the bazaar. At night, there are some of the most respectable harem dancers in the floor shows that you've ever seen."

He narrowed his eyes thoughtfully. "You make it sound as if you were going to Cincinnati for the weekend."

"If you were a true New Yorker," she teased, "you'd say going out west to Cincinnati."

"You have a point there." Josh swallowed the rest of

his drink and put his empty glass on the end table. "Does all this wanderlust indicate an inability to settle down? Or don't the men in Weehawken and Brooklyn rate your attention?"

Her slight blush showed that his jibe had scored. "Locale has nothing to do with it. As you well know."

"I know that your 'simple kindness' philosophy can only work so far. Very few men have the ability to make Hoboken look as good to a woman as a summer palace on the Bosphorus. You'd better not expect miracles," Josh announced calmly.

"I don't," she said through stiff lips. "There's no use continuing this discussion. I told you we were wavelengths apart."

"Dammit, I've done it again, haven't I?" He raked his fingers through his hair in vexation. "If I apologize, will you promise not to set the cat on me?"

She laughed outright. "Of course. It might be better if we changed the subject, though. You were going to tell me what was going on at the office."

"Hasn't Mark kept you informed on Forcada's condition?"

"He said that he's doing as well as can be expected."

"Another medical cliché," Josh said, "but that's the story. In one of Emilio's lucid moments, he claimed no knowledge of his assailant. Apparently he was timing this new poetry program and had his back to the door."

"And the volume level on the playback was probably turned way up." Jane shifted on the couch to tuck her feet up under her before continuing. "He keeps it so noisy when he's timing that I doubt if he'd hear an atom bomb."

"That's what I told Lieutenant Nolan. Incidentally, he gave this script back to us to keep for Forcada." Josh reached in his coat pocket to pull out some flimsy sheets and handed them to Jane. "The lieutenant mentioned that you'd gone over it with him the night Emilio was hurt."

"Yes, I remember." She thumbed through them slowly. "I told him it looked as if Emilio had just been doing research for his program."

"Anita Warren backed you up. She said Forcada was all enthused over the poetry idea and had been working harder than usual on his script."

"Where was Anita when all this happened?"

"Off duty. She had put in extra time lately, so she was given compensating time off. Madge Waverly knew about it; I imagine even Fred Hall had been told. It was down on the scheduling sheets for anyone to check."

"So if this wasn't a spur of the moment thing . . ." Jane frowned as her voice trailed off.

He nodded. "Let's say that our attacker could be pretty sure of having the library to himself just by taking a quick look at the schedule. Of course, he or she had to run the risk of an announcer coming by to drop off some records."

"But even that could have been covered by going in during the programs rather than at the half or quarter hours." She leaned over the coffee table and put her wine glass on a coaster. "Of course, there would always be the chance of some interruption, but I shouldn't think the risk would be too great."

"You're assuming that whoever it was belonged in the department." Josh was watching her carefully but remained relaxed against his cushion.

"Why, yes, I suppose I am." She gave him a quick glance. "Isn't that the way the official thinking is going?"

He shook his head. "As suspects, International personnel are 'also-rans' at the moment. Lieutenant Nolan has found that Forcada was up to his ears in Caribbean politics. Those customers play rough even in this country. That's why there's a hospital guard on Forcada, and now that his wife has flown in to be with him, the police are very conscientious indeed. Our State Department knows that if some hothead took a shot at her while she's here, our national image would suffer in the Caribbean."

"Which translates to?"

"Her papa would start accepting foreign aid from the other side. That's the reason for the furor; there must be more State Department staff watching her than the Russian teletypes."

"I hope you didn't come to International expecting a rest," Jane remarked soberly.

"Take that look off your face, Miss Chapin. Don't forget we have a temporary truce."

"So we have." She leafed absently through the script again.

"Anything interesting in it?"

"Well, if you like poetry, Emilio's chosen his selections well. He has works by Rubén Darío, José Chocano, and Alfonso Reyes." She was examining the pages closely. "He's even included Leopoldo Lugones—a favorite of mine."

Josh slid along the couch to look. "You'll have to translate for me."

His sudden nearness made her take a firmer grip on the flimsy sheets. "Are you sure you're interested?" In her determination to appear casual, her voice took on a curt note.

His eyebrows shot up. "I wouldn't have asked otherwise."

"Very well. The translation is rough, don't forget."

"You're perfectly safe," he assured her. "Don't you forget that my Spanish is practically nonexistent."

"Emilio has just a fragment of this one. . . . It goes 'The blue sky was fragrant with rosemary and in the deep fields the pheasant was whistling . . .'" She studied the script carefully. "It looks as if he was using it for a lead-in with music underneath. The next one is in a more sombre vein. 'And at our feet, a river of hyacinths ran noisily toward death.' Seems to be a coincidence, doesn't it? Here he has picked one of the better known works." She indicated a place on one of the pages. "I'll just translate the last part."

And little by little, the fatal thread was
    unwinding itself.
No longer did I retain it, except one end
    between my fingers.
When suddenly you became cold and no longer
    kissed me.
And I let go the end and life left.

There was a silence between them as her soft voice stopped. "It's quite lovely," she said finally. "Frankly, I shouldn't have thought it was Emilio's meat, at all."

"It's interesting you should say that," Josh said quietly. "I was thinking the same thing about the verse in English that he has included."

"I know the one you mean." She rifled through the pages. "Here it is . . . the one that starts 'Send home my harmless heart againe.' I'm afraid I don't recognize it." She handed the script back to him. "Spanish or English, they're all in the same vein."

"He must have been beaming the program for a feminine audience."

She smiled in response. "You mean a two-handkerchief show where the women can have a lovely weep."

"Exactly."

"You're probably right. Can I offer you another drink?"

"No, thanks. I'll be going so that you can get ready for your dinner date."

"Don't hurry," she murmured politely.

"I haven't." He stood up and looked around. "Where's the beast?"

"Fig?" She walked to the hallway and peered into the bedroom door. "You're safe," she reported, coming back. "The terror of the twelfth floor is sitting on a bureau looking out the window."

"You might try leaving the window open and seeing if he'll jump."

"Don't be bitter," she said with a gamine smile. "Otherwise, he'll hear you and come back for another go-round."

"The dialogue sounds familiar, so this must be where I came in." Josh straightened his tie. "Thanks very much for the drink."

"And thank you for the dinner invitation." She bit her lip and then said, "Seriously, if that bite of Fig's gives you any difficulty . . ."

"Should I call a lawyer or a doctor?" Josh asked gravely. Too gravely.

"The doctor." She kept her voice as solemn as his. "I'm the one who should call a lawyer in case you sue me. Do you suppose my liability policy covers this?"

"Nobody is insured against all risks. You'll have to take your chances from now on." Josh's penetrating glance moved from her head to her toes and back again.

He took his time about it before he said, "I like a challenge. Makes life interesting."

Her cheeks had flushed under his masculine scrutiny. "Why don't you try something like climbing the Matterhorn and leave me out of it?"

"I think you might have as many complications," he said judicially. "Usually bundles of naïveté don't come wrapped in such a beautiful cover."

Her flush deepened. "You'd better go, Mr. Blake. I'm not as naïve as you might think."

He winked as he opened the door. "Don't bet on it, Miss Chapin—I'd hate to take your money. At any rate, we shall see."

# Chapter Five

❦ ❦ ❦

Late summer humidity was making itself felt with a vengeance the next morning when Jane returned to work.

"Wouldn't you think they'd learn to regulate these air conditioners better?" Horrie Cole complained when he stopped by her desk. "If I expire of heat prostration, they just revive me in time to make my next show."

Jane looked up from the crossword puzzle she'd saved from the morning paper. "If you want to expire, use the couch. It won't be here much longer, so we should take advantage of it."

"This is more like it," Horrie said fervently, sinking down on the leather. "You can wake me in half an hour."

"If you're that badly off, maybe you should see Dr. Jamieson," she replied, distracted momentarily from a four-letter word meaning Goddess of Harvests.

"I'll be fine if you'll just pipe down."

Jane ignored his protest. "Seriously, you look terribly

tired. This is no time for you to be under the weather. You'll need all your strength in a little while for those two o'clock feedings."

"Don't I know it!" He sounded bitter. "Unfortunately I can't get it across to my wife. She can't sleep in this heat and likes conversation with her insomnia."

Jane smiled despite herself. "You are in a bad way."

Horrie stretched luxuriously on the couch. "I did get a small measure of revenge."

"How?" she asked idly.

"I kept falling asleep in the middle of my answers."

"You're sadistic," she informed him, picking up her pencil again.

"You are so right." Tom Carmichael was grinning at them from the doorway. "I've been telling him so for years."

Horrie pushed up on an elbow and then subsided again. "Tell him to go away, Janie. Far—far—away."

"Don't disturb our production chief," she parroted faithfully. "He's in a bad way. Or so he says."

"If I enter this in my log," Tom said, matching her tone, "what do I put down as the cause of the trouble?"

"Exhaustion," Horrie managed to quaver. "Brought on by overwork. Extreme overwork."

Tom and Jane's laughter brought Madge Waverly on the scene. "A little more noise, my loves," she said, "and you'll interrupt the conference that Mr. Hall and Josh Blake are holding with the State Department guru. Somebody's head will roll, I'm warning you."

"Are they in Mr. Hall's office now?" Jane asked in a lowered tone.

Madge nodded. "Something to do with Emilio, I suppose."

"Sorry, Madge," Tom put in. "We didn't know."

"That's all right, I was just kidding," Madge replied. "You weren't making *that* much noise. I came to ask a favor—will you answer my phones while I go downstairs and rustle some coffee for the great men?"

Tom frowned and glanced at his watch. "Officially, I'm off duty until this afternoon, but if you won't be long . . ."

"Go ahead," Jane told Madge, who hesitated. "I'll be here and I'll be glad to take any messages until you come back."

"Thanks, Jane." Madge flicked her a grateful wave. "Shan't be long!"

"I'm sorry to inconvenience you, Janie," Tom said after Madge disappeared down the hall. "I promised to drop in on my sister, and visiting hours are strict."

She nodded in sympathy. "Of course, I understand. I didn't realize she was still in the hospital."

"I'm hoping she'll be out soon. Sometimes I think her doctor is hanging crepe so he can add more to the bill."

"Surely not," she said gently. "Hospital rooms are in such short supply from what I've heard that doctors are happy to get their patients home again."

"Nuts! I could tell you some stories—"

"Why don't you pipe down or go somewhere else," Horrie said from the couch. "If I want to hear an argument, I can go home and listen to my wife. You're disturbing my rest."

"If you don't like it, you know damned well what you can do about it," the traffic manager flared back.

"Stop it, Tom." Jane pulled him toward the hallway. "It must be the weather. We're all at each other's throats."

He yanked away. "What do you mean by that?"

"Well, what do you think? Horrie's trouble is a lack of sleep. What's yours?" she asked in a crisp tone.

"I don't have any trouble," he replied belligerently. "Except for those lousy college courses. There's a quiz I should be studying for right now." His shoulders sank as if he'd received a blow.

"Go study for your quiz and you'll feel better," Jane said, concerned by his depression. "And we'll let Horrie sleep so he'll feel better."

"A lack of sleep isn't all that's wrong with him. He's bothered by this Forcada mess more than he'll admit."

Jane turned up a bewildered face. "Why should the attack on Emilio affect Horrie? More than the rest of us, I mean?"

"If you'd worked here longer, you'd know," Tom said evasively.

"That isn't any answer. I don't think you should say things like that—it isn't fair to Horrie."

"I'm not running out to tell Lieutenant Nolan," Tom said, sounding sullen. "It isn't any secret to the rest of us that Horrie's on the other side of the political fence from Forcada. He's never bothered to hide it."

"I didn't know Horrie was even interested in politics."

"People who've lived in the Caribbean have more than a little interest in what's happening there." He stared at her. "You should know what I mean."

"When I worked in a foreign country, I was careful to stay away from local politics. That was the first thing you learned."

"You and Josh Blake. He must have saddle sores by now from straddling political fences."

She stepped back. "I can only think that you wouldn't do very well on the diplomatic front this morning, Tomás, my friend. Why don't you go along before you say anything else."

"Janie, I'm sorry!" He caught her hand between his

palms. "I didn't mean to make you mad. It's just that I'm in a filthy mood this morning—probably comes from working that early shift." His hold tightened. "Say you'll forgive me."

"By all means, say you'll forgive him, Miss Chapin." Josh paused by them on the way to his office. "Or pick another place for the tender renunciation scene."

"It isn't anything like that," Tom put in defensively. "I was trying to apologize."

"Spare me the details," Josh said, bestowing a bleak look on both of them. "Have you seen Horrie lately?"

Jane sneaked a look back down the hall toward the couch before she could stop herself. Josh frowned as her gesture became clear but didn't comment directly.

"When you see him again," he said, emphasizing the first word, "tell him I need his opinion on the script for the new Portuguese show. Can you manage that, Miss Chapin?"

She didn't let his sarcasm put her off that time. "Of course, Mr. Blake. If I don't see him before Madge gets back, I'll pass the message on."

Josh let his glance go down the hallway again but he merely said, "Thanks very much," and disappeared into his office.

Tom stared after him. "He'd better have the next shift on the couch after Horrie. I wonder what his trouble is?"

"I have a damned good idea," Horrie said, coming around the corner and smoothing his hair to a semblance of order, "but I'd better not say with a lady present."

"You heard?" Jane asked.

"Oh, man, did I hear! I'd better get on that script or my unborn child will find himself with an unemployed father." He sighed and scratched the back of his neck. "I forgot all about it—the script, I mean."

Tom groaned. "Don't explain your so-called wit."

"Oh, darn," Jane's voice trailed off as she looked at Blake's tightly closed office door. "Speaking of forgetting, I wanted to tell him . . ."

"What?" Horrie interrupted lazily, moving toward his office.

"That he'd left a script of Forcada's at my apartment. I meant to bring it along and give it back to him."

Cole stopped in mid-stride and stared. "You mean the great man has been calling on you?"

"I could have told you that," Tom contributed, watching Jane's discomfiture with enjoyment. "Evidently you didn't have a softening effect on his emotions, Janie, or was he just making a regulation sick call?"

"I didn't ask," she began, only to have Horrie interrupt again.

"Madge says he likes pale, expensive-type blondes," he informed her. "That's the way it goes, *rojita linda*. If you play fickle with me and Tom . . ."

"Plus the good Dr. Jamieson," Carmichael added with sarcasm.

"You'll end up watching the late movie all by yourself," Horrie finished.

"When I worked in South America," Jane said, "the revolutions and the snipers only lasted three days. I must say it was good training for this place." She fixed Horrie with a severe glance. "But if you don't get on with that script, Josh Blake will be starting a private war before the day is over. This time, I'm on his side."

Fortunately all the minor skirmishes had been resolved by the time Mark Jamieson called for her later that evening.

"Don't tell me you're actually ready and waiting," he said in pleased surprise as he strode into the foyer of her apartment building to pick her up for their dinner date. "I thought that only happened on television or in the movies."

She smiled up at him. "In the movies, the hero is always allotted a half block of parking space. I didn't think you'd be so lucky."

"I never am. That's why I have a cab waiting outside—conveniently doubleparked."

She subsided thankfully in the taxi, waiting until he shut the door and gave an address to the driver before she said, "Going out to dinner is marvelous! By far the best thing that's happened all day."

"Was it a grim one?"

"Terrible. Probably because I forgot to read my horoscope in the paper this morning. At least then I would have been warned."

"It can't have had much effect—you look too good now. Like a page out of a fashion magazine," he said, letting his glance travel over her admiringly. The cocktail dress of ecru lace clung to her trim figure in all the right places, with the boat-shaped neckline providing a flattering frame for her shoulders and throat. She'd draped a green silk topcoat around her shoulders and wore matching sandals.

"I don't know whether it's that green coat or those dangle earrings," Mark went on, "but you're raising my blood pressure."

"You must need rest and relaxation, Doctor," she teased.

"Just what I have in mind. Along with holding hands all the way across town."

She tucked her envelope purse beside her and gravely offered him a hand. " 'Hand in hand, with wand'ring steps and slow—through Eden took their solitary way,'" she quoted. "John Milton had the idea long ago."

He took her slender fingers and held them gently in his bigger ones. "I wonder," he mused, "if anyone ever thought to look for Eden on Fifth Avenue in the late summer."

She tightened her grip in a quick, understanding movement. "Let's try, Mark. Sometimes all you can do is try."

The restaurant he'd chosen was popular and looked as if it should be tucked away among the palm trees of Hawaii rather than occupying most of the upper floor in a Manhattan skyscraper.

They stepped from an express elevator into an atmosphere of lush tropical greenery and bright Polynesian colors whose vibrant tones were only partially subdued by the concealed lighting. A suave maître d'hôtel emerged to hover expectantly beside them, and at a murmured word from Mark, he led them to a banquette placed so that they could enjoy an almost unobstructed view of the East River and sections of Brooklyn and Queens. His place was swiftly taken by a petite Japanese girl clad in a colorful kimono and obi who waited for their order.

Jane smiled at Mark. "Do you mind making the decisions?"

"Not at all. I take it there's nothing you're violently against? No allergies?" As she shook her head, he ordered champagne cocktails and reserved mahi-mahi for their dinner. "It's flown in daily from Hawaii," he explained, "and so popular that it's best to speak up early."

Their champagne cocktails arrived promptly in fragile-stemmed glasses.

"What should we drink to?" Mark asked, lifting his glass. Jane gave a little laugh and carefully touched the edge of her glass to his. "Happiness, of course." Her voice was slightly unsteady as an unbidden picture of Josh Blake suddenly appeared in her mind. She recalled how intent his glance had been as he'd sat in her living room the day before, the gentle cynicism in his voice as he'd raised his glass in a toast.

"Hey, lady. Come on back." Mark sounded slightly ruffled. "You look as if you'd left for another continent already. I hope you're not bored with my company so early in the evening."

"Of course not." She took a hasty sip of her drink. "Umm—lovely. Just like the surroundings. I was wool-gathering for a moment," she went on apologetically, and then looked around puzzled as music started close by. "Where have they hidden the combo?"

He laughed, his irritation clearly forgotten. "It's tucked around the corner, next to the usual postage-stamp floor for dancing. We can move over there for coffee and liqueurs after dinner." He paused before adding, "I'll be glad to take you once around the floor but I'm a total loss as a dancer."

"That's all that's needed. After the dinner you've ordered, I'll scarcely be able to move." She sighed and rested her head against the cushioned banquette. "It's nice to sit here and relax. Especially after all the furor in International today."

"I suppose this Forcada thing has them more upset than usual." Mark concentrated on eating the orange slice impaled on a plastic drink stirrer. "At least, that's what Josh says."

"He's scarcely one to talk." Her tone was indignant. "You'd better prescribe some tranquilizers for him. He can be ruder without trying than anyone I've ever met."

Mark managed a wry grin. "Why all the indignation? At least he seems to have made some kind of an impression on you, which is more than I've accomplished."

"Now that's being silly." Her voice softened. "Meeting you and getting to know you has been one of the nicest things that's happened to me during my stay in New York."

He covered her hand for just a moment and then released it with a sigh. "That doesn't sound like the thing a heroine says to the hero before they ride off into the sunset together."

She burst out laughing. "If I know you, the heroine would have to run competition with those test tubes in your laboratory. In fact, I'll bet she'd be hard pressed to get your attention most of the time."

He grinned in response and rubbed the back of his neck ruefully. "I'm beginning to be a changed man. Even Josh noticed the difference."

"I didn't think he had time to notice things like that."

Mark's eyebrows rose. "You sound bitter. Don't tell me he's losing his touch. I had disgruntled women weeping on my shoulder when he and I were roommates in college."

"Was that because he favored them with his attentions or because he didn't?"

Mark ignored her sarcasm, saying merely, "They came to me for advice after they lost out with Josh. I must say"—his tone was almost smug—"I certainly made the most of it."

She pretended to look apprehensively over her shoulder. "Be careful. You'll be blacklisted by every women's group in town."

"Sorry." Mark didn't sound worried and his glance was unabashed. "Don't forget, that was a few years ago. These days, I'm a pillar of responsibility. So is Josh—at least to hear him tell it."

"Maybe that's his fatal fascination."

Mark shrugged. "Maybe. There's also quite a bit of money in his family. I think Josh always felt that spurred the chase for most of his dates when he was in college. Actually, I think most women were attracted to him because he was hard to get. He'd squire a good-looking gal for a month or so and then take up with another one. Maybe he still does."

"I can't see why any woman in her right mind would be attracted to a man who behaved like that." Jane failed in her attempt to sound casual and she knew it as soon as the words were out.

Mark wasn't deceived. "Women always hanker for the unobtainable," he said. "You know it, so do I."

"Don't count on it. Sugar is still the best come-on for the female of the species, Doctor."

"Well, salt didn't hurt Josh's chances. As a matter of fact, you're the first woman I've heard complain about his rudeness. Lack of interest, yes—but as for losing his temper, I don't think he generally bothers."

"And that's a left-handed compliment if I ever heard one. I can't imagine any normal woman being attracted to a man who only cares about the group rate."

"Grow up, Jane. You can hardly expect any male in Josh's age group not to have known and admired several women along the way. If you don't acknowledge it, you're closing your eyes to reality." Mark paused to look at her more closely. "Or maybe there's something in your past that makes you sensitive."

"I knew it!" She struck her palm against her forehead dramatically. "It was absolutely bound to happen."

"Knew what?" he asked, alarmed.

"That you couldn't resist dragging in a psychiatrist's couch." She eyed him severely. "No dice, Doctor. There's nothing wrong with my libido, and I'm not nursing a grievance just because I refuse to wait in line for some man to decide whether I fit his mood of the moment."

Mark winced at her words. "Caught in my own trap. Well, if I can't get you to the psychiatrist's couch, how about another cocktail?"

"You needn't be devious and try to change the subject, either."

"I thought you were tired of that particular one," he teased.

"All right—so I'm curious. I may not approve of your behavior during college, but I'd still like to know what happened afterward."

"To me—or to Josh?"

"Both of you," she admitted, knowing that she'd hadn't fooled him one iota.

"It would serve you right if I took you at your word," he said sternly. Then his tone relaxed. "After undergraduate work, Josh went to law school. In due course, he was admitted to the bar and put in some time for Uncle Sam in the Pacific on the adjutant general's staff. Toward the end of his army stint, he was stationed in Washington, D.C. I suppose that's why he began his civilian practice there. I know he's been doing lots of work for Continental and they'd like to put him on an exclusive retainer. That could mean moving here permanently. I imagine his father would be delighted to have him share the family apartment."

"Is it an exclusively masculine domain?"

"If that's a subtle inquiry," he said drily, "you needn't go to so much trouble. Just let me know the details I've missed in this saga."

Color rose in her cheeks. "Very well. What happened to Mrs. Blake?"

"Josh's mother? She died when he was in prep school. His father has never remarried. A few years ago, he retired from his corporate law practice and now he spends most of his time traveling. I think he's in Hong Kong at the moment. Speaking of traveling, don't you think you've had your quota?" Mark put his hand over hers on the table with a possessive gesture. "My love, you could pick your job if you stayed with me. I'd even take you on at the office—that's if you can't be persuaded to share a marriage license after we get to know each other a little better. I'm not fooling now," he said as he saw the astonishment on her features.

"I know." For a moment, she couldn't go on. Then she gave his fingers an affectionate squeeze. "You make me feel like such a terrible fizzle, Mark, dear. If I had an ounce of sense, I'd accept your offer so fast that you wouldn't have a chance to realize your mistake."

"That means it's no go." His mouth twisted as he tried to make the best of an awkward pause. "Thank god, you didn't add that chestnut about 'being friends.' "

"You're much too tempting for the 'friends' category," she said frankly. "It's probably just as well that I'll be leaving town shortly or I might make an awful fool of myself."

"Hey, cut that out. What will the management think if they see you in tears," he chided her. "I shouldn't have even mentioned it tonight. After working at Continental, you'd think I'd have a better sense of timing."

"That's right." She'd found her handkerchief by then and used it before turning to smile tremulously. "Horrie would have a fit—probably even give you a stopwatch."

Mark nodded. "I see our dinner approaching. At least, that's right on cue. Nothing should get in the way of mahi-mahi." He lifted his champagne glass. "Let's enjoy the calories and let our emotions fend for themselves."

Later that evening, they were escorted to another table on the edge of the dance floor and gave their order for coffee and liqueurs.

"I can't think why I've never visited Hawaii," Jane murmured as she watched the musicians, who were wearing bright patterned shirts, throw themselves feverishly into an instrumental medley. "If it's even partly like this, you'd be tempted to stay there forever." She turned to survey Mark fondly. "This has been a wonderful evening. Thanks for bringing me."

"We're still in the shank of it. Let's try the dance floor. Anything more current than this kind of a foxtrot leaves me out in left field." He stood up and reached for her hand. "I should take some lessons— Well, what do you know!" He broke off in mid-sentence as he sighted a couple being brought to a table nearby. "It's Josh and that gorgeous gal of his." He cast an apprehensive glance at Jane, who had frozen in her chair. "Would you rather leave?"

"Of course not." She raised her head to greet the other two as they came by the table. "Good evening."

Ellen Barton inclined her chin the required half-inch in greeting and tightened her fingers on the sleeve of Josh's dinner jacket. "Miss—er—Chapin, isn't it?" Her smile appeared briefly. "I hope you're feeling better. How nice to have Mark by your side in case of a relapse."

A flush surged to Jane's cheekbones at the innuendo. "I'm feeling fine, thank you. Good evening, Mr. Blake."

"Good evening, Miss Chapin." Was there an amused undertone on his last two words? It was hard to tell; his features were devoid of expression as he looked down at her. "I didn't know anyone could persuade Mark to leave his test tubes for a night on the town."

"Janie could persuade me to do most anything," Mark informed him. "Will you join us?"

"Thanks, we'd be glad to," Josh replied.

It seemed to Jane that a momentary expression of pique flitted over Ellen Barton's thin lips as she sat down and carefully arranged her wispy black chiffon stole. Her dress was cut in a daring décolleté of the same material but cleverly draped in soft folds from the shoulders to remain in perfect taste. Not a strand of her silver gilt hair strayed from the perfection of her coiffure and she wore diamond earrings to match the diamond brooch at her shoulder.

Jane watched as Josh bent to light the woman's cigarette and found herself wincing at the sight of those two sleek heads so close together.

"Mark, I hope you can persuade Josh not to rush home," Ellen said after sitting back. "After all, this is a celebration."

"Something special?" Mark asked.

Jane's throat tightened as she waited for Ellen's reply.

"Just my birthday, worse luck." Ellen reached in her square evening bag and pulled out a thin cigarette case exquisitely made of black morocco leather trimmed in gold. "Look at the lovely present Josh gave me. Hasn't he wonderful taste?" Her clipped voice went on. "I told him that I deserved a drink with him after we put up with the rigors of a family dinner."

"I hope we didn't spoil your plans," Mark said politely.

"Don't be silly," Josh put in. "If Ellen hadn't twisted my arm, I'd be halfway home by now. Frankly, I'm beat."

"I thought you looked tired at work," Jane put in artlessly. "Maybe you haven't been getting enough rest. Horrie told me some statistics that apply to men in their mid-thirties . . ."

Mark choked on a swallow of coffee and looked across the table at her, his eyes watering. "I think that's a rhumba, Jane," he managed in a stifled tone. "Let's see if I can remember how." He took her arm in a firm grasp, nodded their excuses to the other two, and led her onto the floor. "Now what are you trying to do to the man," he asked as they mingled with the other dancers. "Hand him to the woman on a silver salver?" He tightened his grip around her waist and swung her out of the way of an oncoming couple. "Mid-thirties, indeed! You should have seen the look he gave you."

"I did," she confessed in a small voice. "The trouble is, he has no sense of humor."

"I'm not so sure. We might have found out if I hadn't pulled you out onto the dance floor so fast." He nodded his head toward a couple moving in perfect rhythm on the opposite side of the floor. "For a tired, middle-aged man, he looks damned good on a dance floor."

"Oh, Mark, stop teasing." She bit her lower lip hard. "You needn't commiserate with the man. I'm sure the elegant Miss Barton is doing plenty of that."

"Why, Janie." He stopped for a minute in the middle of the floor and looked at her. "As bad as that? I didn't know."

"Isn't it ridiculous?" she said unsteadily. "If I don't watch out, I'll be just like all those other darned idiots standing in the line. I don't think I realized the effect he had on me until he walked into the room a few minutes ago. Then I found myself wanting to indulge in a hair-pulling match with that gorgeous blonde creature, so I knew I must be farther gone than I had realized." She gave a shaky little laugh. "Wouldn't you think I'd know better than to be attracted by someone who seems to have spent the better part of his life beating off bedazzled women."

"Now listen," Mark protested, "you're not being fair to Josh. Although," he murmured almost to himself, "why I'm building him up in your eyes is more than I can understand. Anyhow, you can hardly blame the man for being an innocent bystander. He certainly didn't encourage any of the ones I knew." Mark looked across the dance floor again. "Ellen might be a different story, though. She certainly acts possessive—maybe with reason."

"I'll have to leave . . ." Jane said softly.

"You mean now?" Mark frowned.

"No, I'm talking about work. There's no need for me to put in the final weeks at International. I've done all the pressing things, and Uncle Fred can hire somebody else to finish up." She glanced up appealingly. "Maybe you could persuade him to transfer me up to your department."

"That could be done easily. Besides"—his smile was smug—"I'd get to see a lot more of you that way."

She smiled in response. "That's nice of you. Actually, it might be better for everyone concerned if I just folded my tent and went on to the west coast."

"Things aren't that serious yet." As the music stopped, he held her quiescent against him and looked around at the emptying dance floor. "Guess it's an intermission. That means I'll have to relinquish my rights momentarily." He guided her back toward their table at the edge of the floor.

Ellen was in the midst of a conversation with Josh, who rose to his feet as they approached. The chairs had been shifted while they were away so that Ellen was flanked by the two men and Jane found herself at the end of the group next to the dance floor. Josh held her chair and sat down beside her.

Mark looked helplessly across the table before inclining his head to hear what Ellen was saying.

"You needn't worry," Josh told Jane calmly as she reached for her coffee; "Mark isn't going to be diverted very long." As the relief musicians came in to pick up their instruments and launched into a smooth rhythm number, he added, "This sounds pretty good. Shall we?" His insistent hand at her elbow precluded a reply.

"It's nice that I didn't plan to refuse," she murmured irritably as he led her onto the dance floor. "Considering I wasn't given a chance."

"I get the feeling you don't approve of Ellen's methods or mine."

Jane met his enigmatic gaze levelly. "Does it matter?"

"That depends."

"I'll admit they're expedient. Maybe not in the rule book, but so long as you understand each other," she shrugged, "that's all that matters."

"Could it be that you don't appreciate competition?" he asked, unperturbed.

"That isn't it. I don't mind honest competition." Her lips quirked. "Maybe I'm out of my class. They don't usually allow novices in with the more experienced animals."

"We're not discussing dog and cat shows."

"Aren't we?"

His mouth curved in an unwilling smile and his clasp at her waist tightened as the musicians went into a lilting encore. "I won't accept that novice description. Every time I see you, you have a different man in tow."

"You don't look like a candidate for monastic life," she countered, "so you can't be objecting."

"Oh, I'm not," he assured her. "Older men in the mid-thirties have to take all they can get. That's a direct quote in case you've forgotten." His manner sobered suddenly. "Right now, I'm more interested in other things. Has Lieutenant Nolan been around to ask you any questions recently?"

"No." She looked up at him, puzzled. "Should I have expected him?"

"I'm not sure. I think he's keeping a weather eye on all of us. The guard is still on duty in Forcada's room at the hospital, too."

She frowned at hearing that. "Do you really think he expects any action there?"

"I don't know about that, but ̶ ̶ ̶ ̶ ̶ ̶ ̶ ̶ ̶ national gets any more unsa̶ ̶ ̶ ̶ ̶ ̶ ̶ ̶ gressional appropriation will ju̶ ̶ ̶ ̶ ̶ ̶ ̶ ̶ critics are standing in line to l̶ ̶ ̶ ̶ ̶ ̶ ̶ days. Fred Hall and I are g̶ ̶ ̶ ̶ ̶ ̶ ̶ ̶ing for the diplomatic corps if we ever ne̶ ̶ ̶ ̶ ̶ ̶ ̶ange jobs."

"Blessed are the peacemaker̶ ̶ she began.

"Even if they're not pur̶ ̶ of heart," he finished promptly. "It doesn't seem to ̶ elp me when I get in a knock-down, drag-out with yo̶ ̶ I wonder why?"

"You'd better ask Mark. H̶ ̶ might have an afternoon free if you feel like psychiatric consultation."

Josh winced. "There you go again."

"Sorry. Let's get off the subject. I meant to tell you that you left Forcada's script at the apartment."

"So I did." His smile reappeared. "Are you issuing a return invitation?"

"You'd be very welcome" she said smoothly, "but I'll leave it on your desk tomorrow. That way, you'll be sure to get it." As the music blared to a finale, she added, "Thank you for the dance."

He caught her elbow before she could start toward

their table. "Hold on a minute. There's no need for you to be in such a tearing hurry to get back to Mark. I wanted to tell you that I'll have to break this up."

"It's a shame that you and Miss Barton have to leave so early."

"I can tell that you're completely devastated by the prospect." His jaw firmed ominously. "We never get the air cleared between us. Everytime we start acting like human beings and achieve a truce, something blows it sky-high."

"In that case, you'd better leave things alone," Jane said, staring determinedly over his shoulder.

"Why?"

She freed her elbow from his grasp and started slowly toward their table. "Do you have to have a reason for everything? Just take my word for it."

He glared down at her as they came to the table. "If I couldn't think of a better excuse than that, I'd give up."

"Josh, there's no need to be rude to Miss Chapin." Ellen sounded amused as she broke the silence following his remark. "Not everyone would tolerate such rudeness."

"Come on, Ellen," Josh said, ignoring her rebuke. "I'm sorry to break this up, but I still have some work to finish at home. It's been nice seeing you, Mark," He shook hands with Jamieson, who had been a silent onlooker to the conversation after seeing that Jane was made comfortable.

Ellen looked annoyed, but she reached for her purse and stood up. "At least, I demand a cab ride through the park if you're dragging me home so early, Josh." She spared a glance toward Jane. "Good night, Miss Chapin. I'm glad you're looking better." Mark rated a brilliant smile. "It was so nice being with you—we'll have to do it again."

Mark nodded as he got to his feet and watched them leave. He waited until they were out of sight before he moved over to the chair next to Jane's. He pretended to mop his brow as he said, "Whew! There's one woman who functions on all cylinders. I think I still have enough energy left to manage that rhumba they're playing. Come on, Janie—now that we've lost the competition, let's relax and enjoy life." He reached for her hand and pulled her

He moved her onto the dance floor. "I'll show you—on the way home."

Jane recalled his words as she stepped out of the elevator into her apartment vestibule some time later. Sensing the uncertainty of her mood, Mark had been forced to settle for a lengthy goodnight kiss in the dimly lit foyer of the building before returning to his waiting cab.

She was glad that he'd left without commenting and, not for the first time, wished she could have responded more enthusiastically to the offerings of such a nice man.

Her door key had gravitated to the bottom of her purse and it took a moment or two for her to find it. As she put it in the lock, the ornate door swung in at her touch. "Damn!" she thought; "I must have forgotten to close it tight when I left. I hope to heaven that Fig hasn't gone exploring." She reached for the light switch in the entranceway and stopped, aghast, when she snapped it on.

The living room looked as if it had been hit by gale winds; papers and books from the case in the corner were strewn over the rugs, while cushions from the davenport and chairs were tumbled in the same senseless disorder.

The overturned cocktail tables looked like helpless gilt bugs, extending spidery legs toward the ceiling.

Jane hovered uncertainly in the doorway, wondering what to do first. Her glance focused on the telephone which was still atop its narrow table, although the directory lay face down on the floor with the pages torn and crumpled. Perhaps Uncle Fred could help. Her fingers reached for the receiver and then stopped midway. He had mentioned that he would be playing duplicate bridge at some club tonight. She bit her lip in frustration and tried to think. Mark had mentioned checking on a hospital patient before he returned to his uptown apartment, so there was no telling when he would be available. She glanced again at the littered room in front of her, wondering if she should call the police for that. Suddenly the awareness of being alone in a large city swept over her like a suffocating cloud.

Slowly her hand went out and pulled the telephone directory into its proper place. Her finger searched for a particular number and then, still hesitantly, dialed it on the phone.

"Let him be home," she thought desperately. "Just let him be home."

The buzzing of the receiver sounded again in her ear before it cut out abruptly and a terse masculine voice said, "Blake."

"Josh." She had to clear her throat before she could go on. "It's Jane. I'm sorry to bother you but I need your help—"

"What's the matter?" His tone was brusque as he broke in.

She took a breath, trying to keep her voice steady. "I just got home. Someone's been in here and torn the living room to shreds."

"Take it easy," he soothed. "What about the rest of the place?"

"I don't know. Frankly, I haven't had the nerve to explore." A dull thud sounded in the bedroom and her fingers tightened on the receiver. She laughed nervously. "I just heard Figaro jump to the floor in the bedroom, so I imagine everything's all right."

"If that cat's around"—there was a vestige of humor in his voice—"then I doubt if anyone else is."

. . . . I've been acting like a Victorian heroine with the vapors. Just forget that I called—"

"Don't be silly," he interrupted. "Stay right there and I'll be over. Jane?" He waited for her answer and then said, "Jane!" urgently again.

She heard his voice echoing in her ear as she stared at the black and white figure of the cat, who sat blinking on the rug beside the living room drapery. "Fig—he's in here . . ." She spoke like a sleepwalker. "But the noise was in the bedroom." Slowly her gaze swung to the open bedroom door and fastened with mounting terror on the mirror beside it.

"Jane, are you there?" Josh's voice was raw in her ear. "For God's sake, answer me!"

She tried to speak. All the time that her eyes were fastened on the reflection of that opening closet door, she tried desperately to speak to him. It was only when her mind registered the reflected image of black-gloved fingers emerging stealthily from the closet's gloom that her senses rebelled. Her fingers suddenly went slack to let the receiver smash on the floor, and her knees sagged as the blessed darkness of unconsciousness overcame her.

# Chapter Six

〜 〜 〜

The next things that registered in Jane's mind were a cold, moist substance on her forehead and icy liquid dripping steadily into her ear.

The darkness receded momentarily, long enough to make her yearn for a little padding between her horizontal form and the unyielding affair beneath it. Investigating with her hand, she determined that it was Madam Trimpani's highly polished but nonetheless highly uncomfortable hardwood floor.

"Jane, can you hear me?" It was a worried masculine voice trying to get her attention. "Jane, for lord's sake—wake up!"

Her ear received another icy cascade which forced her eyelids open in protest. "Don't do that," she complained. "I don't want to drown here—not on the floor."

"What are you talking about?"

That time the voice sounded far away. Jane grimaced

and muttered, "I can't hear" as she pushed up on an elbow, trying to shake her head and clear it at the same time. A wave of pain stopped that maneuver abruptly. She groaned and lay back.

"What's the matter? What can't you hear?" The voice was closer but considerably more agitated.

Jane managed to open her eyes again and this time identified a familiar face close to hers. "You've got the ums get artificial respir—resprea—whatever it is. . . ."

"Respiration."

"That's it," she said tiredly. "Not more water."

"Who the hell's drowning?"

"I am." She struggled onto her elbow again and explored her hair with the other hand. "I must be. My ear's so full of water that I can barely hear"—her hand went down to investigate further—"and I'm soaked all over." That made her sit up straighter and she found a strong masculine arm immediately propped behind her shoulders. She winced as the bright overhead light came into her vision. "Lord, my head aches!"

"I know." Josh's voice sounded strangely rough. "It must hurt like the very devil. I'm sorry about getting you so wet—I got too enthusiastic with the water when I was trying to bring you around. Let me help you into the bedroom before I call the doctor."

"Not the bedroom!" It didn't seem possible for her cheeks to blanch any whiter but they did, and she swayed as waves of pain coursed through her head. "There was someone in there. I saw the glove moving on the edge of the door."

"Take it easy. There isn't anyone here now. I checked out the whole place as soon as I arrived." He put a hand under her elbow and helped her up. "Can you manage to stay vertical? Lean on me."

"I'm okay," she said shakily.

"Sure you are, but you're going to bed just the same." His tone eliminated further discussion on that topic.

Jane let herself be led into the bedroom and gingerly sat down on the edge of Madame's oversized mattress.

"Keep that wet cloth on your forehead until the doctor comes. It helps control the bleeding," Josh instructed.

She managed to catch a glance in the mirror on the dressing table opposite. "I must have hit the corner of the telephone table when I fell. All I need is a Band-Aid and some ice to keep the swelling down. If you can get those for me, I won't need to bother any doctor."

"Now wait a minute . . ."

"I mean it." For the first time, she got a clear glimpse of his hand. "It looks as if you could use a bandage, too. You're dripping blood all over your cuff." Her expression suddenly froze with fear. "Josh, you didn't fight with—"

He interrupted her with a disgusted snort as he turned to get the first aid box from the bathroom. "Hell, no! The only thing I tangled with was your cat." He jerked his head toward Fig, who was watching them from the top of a bureau. "Needless to say, I lost again."

Jane bit her lip. "I'm terribly sorry."

"Forget it." Josh emerged with the metal box and opened it to search for antiseptic and bandages. "I think the Defense Department could use him. Or maybe they already have him classified." Josh straightened and came over to sit beside her, bearing the necessary supplies. "Shall I act like the doctor?"

"We can make it a mutual assistance pact." She tilted her head so he could sponge the abrasion on the side of her temple, wincing when he finally applied the strip of bandage. "Ouch! There's no need to be a sadist with that adhesive."

"Sorry, I was thinking of something else." He lowered his hands and gave her an accusing look. "Why in god's name did you hang around and get yourself into a state like this!"

She reached up to smooth the edge of the adhesive so it wouldn't catch her hair. "What did I do wrong *this* time?" By then, she even felt capable of returning a mild glare.

"Well, the obvious thing to do when you came in and found a mess like that in the living room was to turn and walk right out again. Not hang around and wait for something worse to happen."

"Now you're being unreasonable," she told him as she leaned back against the padded headboard. "The worst thing I did was to faint at the crucial moment."

"Use your head, woman," he began impatiently, and then grinned and said, "No, you'd better not. At least, for a while." He screwed the top back on the antiseptic and replaced it in the box before he said, "It's a damned good thing you went out of the picture then. Otherwise you might be keeping Forcada company in the hospital right now."

A cold thread of fear coursed down Jane's back. "You don't honestly think this is related . . ." She broke off and the silence hung between them. Then she swallowed over the thickness in her throat to say, "For heaven's sake, go in and wash the back of your hand and then come back here to let me put some antiseptic on it. You're ruining your handkerchief dabbing at that blood."

He lingered long enough to observe, "You're coming back to normal entirely too fast. All right, I'm going— you're supposed to rest, not raise your blood pressure."

"My blood pressure is perfectly fine."

Josh paused by the bureau and directed a bitter glance at the cat who had settled to nap atop it. "Well, mine's not so hot. If this beast ever sinks a tooth in me again, I swear I'll wring—"

Jane cut in. "Stop bullying him or he'll trip you up before you get the bandage on."

"Over my dead body." The unfortunate words were out before he could stop them and he made an apologetic grimace across the room. "Sorry, I didn't think. I'll be back in a minute. In the meantime, you'd better take off those wet clothes. I hope I didn't ruin your dress with that water." He reached inside the closet door and pulled a quilted robe from a hook on the back of it. "Put this on," he said, tossing it on the end of the bed. "And don't get up to walk around. Can you manage the zippers and things?"

She nodded, feeling her cheeks redden under his amused glance.

"Okay," he said calmly. "Call out when you're receiving again."

Jane swung her legs over the side of the mattress when the bathroom door closed behind him. The movement brought her squarely in line with the half-open closet door and she felt a quiver of fear as her glance lingered on it. What would have happened if she and the intruder had met face to face? Josh was probably right about the fainting spell saving her from a great deal more harm. The only thing she might have gained was knowledge about whether there was any connection between the ransacking of the apartment and the attack on Emilio. Of course, there was a good possibility she wouldn't have been left in a condition to assimilate that knowledge.

"I don't hear any action in there," Josh called out. "Sure you don't need a helping hand."

"I'm sure." She hurriedly pulled the soggy dress over

her head, then dragged the quilted robe around her cold shoulders. Her damp petticoat was the next to go. It would have been nice to slip off her bra and briefs, she thought fleetingly, but it was too complicated to rummage through the bureau drawer for a gown.

"Aren't you ready yet?" The banging of the medicine cabinet punctuated his words. "I'm beginning to feel like a character from some off-Broadway farce stuck in here."

"It's okay now," she called back. "Sorry to have been so long." She tried to pull the lapels of her robe together, both for modesty and to get warmer.

Josh reentered the room, carrying two hot water bottles in front of him. "You'd better have these in bed with you. Madame could damn well use some more heat in this apartment—it feels like an outpost of the North Pole—" He broke off as he surveyed her still figure on the side of the bed. "Why aren't you under the covers?"

"I was just going."

"You bet you are!" With masculine efficiency, he turned back the sheet and blanket, tucking the two bottles toward the foot of the bed. "There, that should do the trick. Now—you're next," he said, turning back to her. "You'd better shed that robe, it looks too bulky to be comfortable under the covers." Before she could start to protest, he had gently shrugged the robe back to reveal her soft and rounded but still cold and damp shoulders covered only by narrow bra straps. "I'll be—" He bit back a savage expletive and yanked the robe around her again. "Are you going out of your way to court pneumonia? Where in hell are your night things?"

Tears rose unbidden to her lashes and she had to swallow before replying. "In that drawer over there—but you told me not to move."

He sat down on the side of the bed and pulled her

tightly against him. "I know. Now relax—in two ticks we'll have you warmed up and into some thick pajamas. Then I'll make you a cup of tea. You're getting the after-effects of shock."

She sighed softly at his comforting words and let herself go limp against his chest. Her head with its tousled damp curls rested over his heart. She discovered, as she lay there, that his breathing suddenly seemed as rapid as hers. In confusion, she started to push back from his clasp.

His arms tightened around her and then, with a rueful laugh, he put her from him and looked down at her with disconcerting frankness. "I thought some 'togetherness' might help, but I don't seem to play the big brother role very well. Actually, I should have known." His fingers bit into the padding of her robe for an instant before he shifted her to a more comfortable position against the headboard. Then he stood up and walked purposefully to the bureau. "Let's find you something sensible to wear."

Jane thought his tone sounded thicker than usual, and her own voice wasn't too steady as she said, "I'm sorry to be such a nuisance. Usually I don't get the whim-whams like this."

"I can imagine." He gave her an appraising glance over his shoulder. "I never thought I'd see a crack in that impenetrable facade of yours."

"You make me sound like Grand Coulee dam," she complained. "And you're certainly lousing up that drawer. I won't be able to find anything," she went on, trying not to sound disconcerted as he held up a filmy nylon gown.

"Very nice," he commented before he replaced it. "But not for now." He rummaged a minute more and then dragged out another. "Here's the very thing. Sensible, old-fashioned flannel, as I live and breathe."

"It was for a hiking trip," Jane said, eyeing the long-sleeved garment with some distaste. For an instant, she wavered between appearances and physical comfort. Then, as a shiver coursed through her, she decided in favor of the latter. She reached over and took the nightgown from him. "Right now, it looks wonderful!"

"Good girl," he said approvingly. "Don't waste any more time. Hop into it and I'll be back in a minute with the tea." He paused in the doorway. "Hot, sweetened tea. They tell me it's very good for shock." There was a strange expression on his face. "I think I'll have some too."

By the time he returned with two steaming mugs, Jane was muffled to the ears in blue flannel.

"This is very nice of you," she said shyly as he put her mug on the bedside table. "I know I shouldn't have bothered you in the first place, but frankly, I couldn't think of anyone else to call."

He waved that aside. "All right if I sit here with you while you drink that tea?"

"Of course." She gestured toward a slipper chair. "That's fairly comfortable. Thank heavens, my landlady decided on upholstered furniture in the bedroom instead of those gilt aberrations. Ummm, this tea tastes good."

"Hope you can stand it with milk and sugar. It sounded more therapeutic that way."

"It's just fine, thanks." Under lowered lashes, she watched him settle in the chair, aware for the first time that he was wearing a sport shirt and gray flannel slacks instead of the dinner jacket she had admired earlier in the evening.

A silence settled between them, but this time, it was a comfortable one which matched the subdued early morning feeling of the city. Even the tea was having a soporific effect rather than a stimulating one, she decided.

"Feel up to talking about it now?" Josh finally asked.

"Of course." She sat more erect and tried to sound as crisp as he did. "There's not much to tell. I came in, found the door ajar, and didn't think too much about it."

"Why was that?"

"Nothing profound." Her lips parted in a smile. "I'm only human. I thought I hadn't latched it when I went down to meet Mark earlier."

"Women!" he said, sounding annoyed. "Were you that excited at having a date with him?"

"That," she said tartly, "is neither here nor there. And certainly none of your business. If you think that coming here gives you the right to sit around and make nasty comments . . ."

"Okay, okay. You don't have to take my head off."

As if his words had suddenly reminded her, Jane put a hand to her bruise, which had again begun to throb with renewed vigor.

Her white, drawn features penetrated Josh's consciousness at the same time. "Oh, lord, Jane—I'm sorry. I don't know why you make me see red all the time. Actually, I shouldn't even be letting you think about what happened. Maybe I'd better call in a doctor for you—just to be on the safe side. There might be a concussion."

"Now you're being silly again." Her voice was softly matter-of-fact and it would have been hard to take offense at the words. "There's nothing wrong with me that sleep won't cure. I'm so warm and comfortable finally that I can hardly stay awake."

He got up to take her empty mug and put it on the bedside table. "One last thing then. Do you remember if anything was missing?"

"Not really. But I don't think so." She wrinkled her forehead, trying to recall. "It looked like pure vandalism—with the chairs overturned and the cushions all over the floor. But to think he was waiting in the closet all the time. . . ." She shuddered visibly and her fingers tightened on the blanket. "Josh, is there a chance he could still be in the building? Waiting for you to leave?"

Josh sat down on the edge of the bed. "Now listen here, my girl," he said, covering her fingers comfortably with his, "trust me, will you?" His expression was stern. "I don't want you to do anything except get some sleep for what's left of the night."

"What will you do?"

"Let me worry about that. Now just slide down and forget about everything." He stood up and reached over to switch off the bedside lamp. "You're perfectly safe now. Nobody's going to hurt you."

She caught at his sleeve for just a moment before her eyes closed and she murmured, "That's the most wonderful thing to hear."

He stood quietly, looking down at her, watching her rapid, shallow breathing gradually deepen as the relaxing sleep took hold. Almost absently, he reached down to pull the blanket more securely around her shoulders. He would have been surprised at the transparency of his expression in that particular moment; at the way he straightened and walked softly out of the bedroom, pulling the door almost closed behind him.

He took a minute to survey the chaotic living room before starting to put things in order. Upended gilt tables were placed back on their legs in the deep-piled scatter rugs. He replaced the cushions on the bulky purple davenport and then knelt to pick up some scattered papers dumped on the floor near a glass-fronted escritoire.

Jane's correspondence had been subjected to a ruthless hand, he decided, as he gathered letters and torn envelopes from the carpet. He hesitated before touching the opened wooden drawers of the writing cabinet and then pushed them back into place decisively. It was a little silly to be considering fingerprints at this late date. He thought once again about calling the police as he returned the bulky Manhattan telephone directory to its rightful place. Lieutenant Nolan would undoubtedly like to hear the latest development, but it was extremely doubtful that Lieutenant Nolan would be in his office at that time of the morning. He glanced again at his watch and yawned reflectively. Amazing how few things were of sufficient interest to awaken anybody at two fifteen in the morning. He eyed the long purple davenport with new interest. Fortunately, it was long enough for a man to stretch out on it. He walked over to the linen closet in the hall which he had noticed earlier and hauled down a blanket and pillow from the top shelf. Dumping them on the couch, he wandered into the kitchen to check the service door. Then he tried the lock on the thick front door and bolted it carefully before reaching for a handy gilt chair to wedge under the doorknob—just in case there were any of the Madame's keys floating around. He walked to the bedroom again and pushed the door open carefully. On tiptoe, he approached the bed and looked at Jane's still figure curled almost in the middle of it. Her breathing sounded all right, he reasoned, and very, very gently he pushed a lock of hair back from her bruised forehead. He felt vaguely reassured even after such a casual contact and tiptoed out of the room, leaving the door wide open this time so that he would hear her if she awakened or cried out.

Wearily, he threw the pillow to one end of the living

room couch and sat down on a purple cushion to remove his shoes. Just then, a rotund black and white figure emerged from behind a living room drape and leaped easily to the far arm of the couch.

"You!" Josh Blake managed to convey a great deal of malevolence in the single word.

Figaro lifted a sturdy black paw and proceeded to survey it carefully, disdaining any interest whatsoever in the room's other occupant.

"That suits me, chum," Josh told him. "Keep your distance or you'll find yourself whisker-to-whisker with this." He hefted one of his shoes suggestively.

Figaro found a new place to wash at the edge of a pink pad on the bottom of his paw. His tongue worked rhythmically and his attention didn't waver.

Josh shook his head and yawned as he punched his pillow into position. Fig stopped his ablutions long enough to match the yawn with one of his own.

The man surveyed him warily as he switched off the light on the end table. With any luck, Josh thought, he'll give me a few hours off for good behavior.

Two minutes later, silence cloaked the room and Fig descended carefully from his perch in the darkness to settle comfortably on a corner of the blanket. After all, there'd be another day.

# Chapter Seven

### ~ ~ ~

Hours later, Josh stirred restlessly, rubbed his nose, and burrowed deeper into the pillow as he tried to ignore a subdued pounding in his ears. The rhythmic thumps accompanied his dream of chasing a platoon of black and white cats down a wide street. His feet were pounding on the pavement and he was relishing the look of abject fear on the feline faces in front of him. Only a few yards more and he'd round them up—show them who was boss.

"Josh! Josh, for heaven's sake—wake up!"

The pounding changed to a shaking and definitely localized in his shoulder. His eyes flew open and he tried to sit up, still more than half-asleep.

"I thought you'd *never* come around," Jane said, exasperated. She was crouched over him by the davenport, with her hair disheveled and the bulky quilted robe dragged on hastily over her flannel gown. One side of the nightgown's collar was bunched over the quilted material,

*111*

giving her a decidedly lopsided effect to his eyes. He blinked again and saw her straighten, casting a desperate look around as the pounding came again—this time from the front door of the apartment. Between knocks, he heard a male voice shouting, "Jane, Jane! Are you all right in there?"

Jane ran a hand through her tousled hair and darted to the door to call through it. "I'll be right there. As soon as I get a robe. Just a minute."

Fortunately that stopped the knocking, and by the time she returned to the davenport, Josh had both shoes on and was trying to fold the blanket.

"Don't bother with that," Jane hissed urgently, stuffing it and the pillow into his arms. "Just throw them into the closet and get into the kitchen. I forgot that Uncle Fred was invited for breakfast."

Josh groaned as he hurriedly dumped the bedding into the linen closet and shut the door. "Dammit, wouldn't you know! This'll go through the department faster than that new Portuguese announcer at quitting time."

"You have it all wrong. I can tell Uncle Fred the truth." She had paused in front of the hall mirror, trying to smooth her hair after settling the collar of her robe. "I'm afraid that he's brought someone with him."

"My god, it's a convention."

"Don't be silly." Her tone was just as terse as his. "Maybe he's alone, but we'd better not take a chance." She gave him an imploring look as she turned toward the front door. "I'm sorry you're involved. Just go in the kitchen and follow my lead later. I wish you'd had time to shave," she added irrelevantly.

"Time to shave!" Josh stopped as if he'd been stung. "If I'd had time to shave, do you think I'd be slinking into the kitchen like some disappointed lover—"

"There's no time for a soliloquy," she flared back. "Will you just get into the kitchen until I find out who's on the other side of the door."

"Sure," Josh said bitterly. "And if it's the Lord Mayor of London—tell him to bring his own crumpets."

Jane watched him disappear behind the kitchen's swinging door and then took a deep breath as she went out into the foyer.

"Jane, dear," Fred Hall bent to kiss her cheek and swept on into the living room as soon as she'd unlocked the door. "I thought you'd forgotten my invitation. No, don't close that," he instructed as he turned and saw her starting to push it shut. "Tom's with me. I sent him for a pass key—no, here he is now."

"Morning, *rojita*," Tom said, as he entered from the vestibule. "Hey, what happened to you?" He put a gentle hand up to the bruise by her temple. "Did you lose or win?"

Fred Hall brushed him aside, his eyes narrowing with concern as he saw the bandage. "My dear, why didn't you say something? What's been going on?"

"Wait a minute—give me a chance." Jane kept her tone light. "When I got home last night, I found a prowler had been here. Oh, it was all right," she said, holding up a hand to forestall their interruptions. "I just slipped on this waxed floor at the crucial moment and hit a table on my way down. It's okay, though—I'll live. No doubt about it."

Tom took her solicitously by the arm. "Gosh, honey, you're in no shape to be worrying about fixing breakfast. You sit down on the couch and I'll bring you some coffee."

"Tom's right," Hall agreed, nodding. "It's no wonder

you were so long answering the door. We must have roused you from a sound sleep."

"Well, not exactly," Jane parried, trying to think of some way to keep Tom from the kitchen other than physically tackling him and finally giving up. "Actually I was awake," she said, making an effort to at least reach the swinging door first and failing in that, too.

"You can't fool me," he joked. "I'd have been sleeping 'til noon if I'd had an experience like that." His voice stopped as abruptly as he did, just inside the kitchen door. "Well, I'll be damned." The last sentence was barely audible.

It did nothing to help the heavy atmosphere as the three of them stood and stared at each other.

"Good morning, Tom." Josh Blake's tone was entirely businesslike as he greeted the other man before he turned to Jane and said, "I've poured the orange juice, but I'm not sure how your coffee maker works so I've left that department to you."

"Oh, fine." Jane tried to instill some light-hearted enthusiasm in her reply. She noted that he had managed to comb his hair in the interval but there was no disguising the morning shadow of beard on his chin. She could only hope that the newcomers would overlook the evidence. "This coffee won't take a minute. Oh, Uncle Fred—" She broke off as the older man pushed open the swinging door and stood staring into the room in surprise. "I meant to tell you," she said, knowing she sounded like something that had been wound too tight, "Josh—er—Mr. Blake is here, too. He came over to answer my S.O.S. last night and then came back this morning." She slowed down to emphasize the last two words before going on brightly, "He wanted to see how I was. Wasn't that kind?"

"Very kind," Fred Hall said. "Nice to see you, Josh."

"It really wasn't necessary. Actually I'm feeling much better today." Jane chattered on, hoping that a steady spate of conversation would distract them. She had a sinking suspicion that her comments were of the "See Jane's lips move" and "Hear Jane talk" variety, but nobody was really listening.

Fred Hall's sharp glance was going over Josh's wrinkled gray flannels and rumpled shirt, finally lingering on the unshaven chin. "Extraordinarily kind of you, Josh—checking on Jane first thing like this. It's reassuring to know you were on the spot—I mean, on the job." His hasty correction showed that he could follow a script, too. For the first time, a slow red streak surged under Josh's cheekbones.

Fortunately Tom missed the byplay. "Why didn't you call the doctor, Jane?" he asked in an aggrieved tone. "You might have been seriously hurt."

"Oh, no. There was nothing that a good night's sleep couldn't take care of." She felt a surge of relief since the awkward moment had passed. "Really, it was perfectly all right."

"Weren't you nervous staying alone?" Tom asked, reluctant to drop the subject.

"But I wasn't—I mean, there wasn't any need to worry," she corrected hastily as Josh almost dropped the can of coffee he had in hand. "Mr. Blake took all sorts of precautions before he—went away," she finished lamely.

"That's right," Josh concurred. He turned to Tom, "I wouldn't have left if I'd thought there was any danger. Give me credit for that."

"Of course," Hall put in. "You're making too much of it, Tom. I imagine Jane would appreciate some peace and quiet rather than a lot of conversation. Tell you what," he added suddenly, "let's leave her and Josh to their coffee and we'll stop off for breakfast on the way to work. I'll even pick up the check."

"But Uncle Fred," Jane protested, "this won't be any trouble."

"No, I insist. I'd ask you to join us but I think you really should be back in bed and I imagine that Josh would prefer to spruce up a bit before appearing in public."

"I certainly would." Josh was definite about that.

"So you see, my dear,"—Hall put an arm around Jane's shoulders as he went back to retrieve his coat and moved toward the front door—"we'll take a raincheck on breakfast and you can tell me all about it later." His tone was pleasant but the expression in his eyes made Jane feel like a five-year-old who had behaved questionably at a birthday party.

"Yes, Uncle Fred."

"See you later, my dear," he said, stooping to kiss her cheek again lightly. "Let's be on our way, Tom."

"All right, if you say so." Carmichael contented himself with a brief squeeze of Jane's hand and a sullen look toward the kitchen. "If you need anything, *rojita* . . ." he began jealously.

"I'll certainly call you." Jane returned the slight pressure of his hand and closed the door rather abruptly behind him. Suddenly exhausted, she let her forehead rest momentarily against the cool wood.

The visit had not been an unqualified success. Obviously Uncle Fred had seen through her pretense and Tom was annoyed that he'd missed out on the excitement. No, that wasn't fair, she decided on thinking it over. Tom had been genuinely concerned. In the past few weeks, she had tried to extend a helping hand and now he was simply trying to reciprocate. It was only natural that he resented

Josh occupying the rescuer's role. Sometime soon she'd have to let him see that friendship was still all she had in mind. With anyone, she told herself firmly, and then wondered why she didn't sound convincing, even to herself.

"I thought you had orders that the next phase was 'back to bed,' " Josh said from the kitchen doorway. "Before you go, though, there are a couple things I have to know. Are you the three-egg type or dry toast and tea?"

"Depends on my mood of the moment," she told him. "But I'm certainly not the 'balance a tray in bed' type. I'd have a relapse trying not to spill the coffee. If you'll sit down and drink your orange juice over there"—she nodded toward the dinette table under a sunny window—"you'll find out that I can even poach an egg."

"Fair enough. I'll manage the toast detail. Incidentally, I figured out how your coffee maker works, so we're halfway home."

"So I see." She concentrated on filling a frying pan with water and put it on the stove. "Did you get the idea we didn't fool Uncle Fred with our story about your early morning sick call?"

He winced and nodded. "I didn't miss the look Tom gave the couch cushions on his way out, either. If we're going to continue playing games, we'll have to be sharper on details."

She carefully broke three eggs into the steaming water and adjusted the heat under the pan. "I know what you mean. Somehow, Uncle Fred will soon manage to get the truth out of me. I'm sure he'll eventually absolve me from our night of sin."

Josh choked violently on his orange juice at that and Jane turned to frown at him. "You needn't collapse. I didn't mean it literally," she announced in a cool tone.

"I'm glad." He had to clear his throat before he could

get the words out. There was irony in his voice when he went on, "I don't usually seduce women in the middle of the week. Especially if they fall asleep while I'm still talking to them." He stared at her thoughtfully. "Even on a good day, you're more the den mother type than the Sadie Thompson model."

"Somehow your compliments never sound like other men's," she said, after a moment's pause. "For that, I think I'll feed Fig his breakfast before you get yours."

"Go ahead. But if he eats here in the kitchen, I hope he chews with his mouth closed. After sharing the couch with him last night, I'd swear he has an adenoid problem."

"He may be listening and decide he'd rather have human flesh than cat crunchies," she warned.

"God forbid." Josh pushed away his empty juice glass and poured a mug of coffee. "I need to be wide awake for this."

Jane smiled impishly over her shoulder as she reached into the top of the broom closet for the cat food. "Any minute, we'll see what happens. Hey—what do you know! Here's Emilio's script." She pulled down a folded handful of papers from the shelf. "I should have returned it to you before this, but I'm getting absent-minded. That's why I stored it with the cat food."

Josh shook his head slowly. "That remark should make sense but it doesn't. All right, Mr. Bones, I'll bite. Why did you put the script with the cat food?"

"Because I always feed Fig in the morning before I go to work and I knew I would remember to get it back to Continental if I put it in the cupboard." She dropped the papers on the table beside him and went back to filling the cat dish.

"I see." He arranged buttered toast slices neatly on the

two waiting plates and then picked up the script sheets and skimmed through them. "I suppose they should go back in the file. Forcada will probably want to keep on with the program when he gets back into circulation."

"Well, he'll certainly have to get back on the payroll if he plans to support Anita *and* his wife. I wouldn't be surprised if he put in for overtime when he's fully recovered." Jane was intent on keeping the yolks intact as she transferred the eggs onto the toast and put the plates in their proper place. "I think that's everything. Can you reach the coffee?"

He nodded and stretched to fill her cup. "Are you hinting that the fair Anita was keeping Emilio on the brink of economic disaster?"

"According to the maestro, Emilio's finances were in such bad shape that he would have had to inquire about an easy payment plan at a second-hand store." She hesitated before adding, "Incidentally, that's pure gossip and I shouldn't be passing it along."

Josh looked amused. "Don't worry. It won't affect Forcada's radio career. I should imagine that if he would reconcile with his wife, he wouldn't have to work at all. It's common knowledge that she receives a healthy stipend from Papa. And if Papa's short of cash, he just dips into the country's treasury."

"That would be handy."

"Yes, indeed. What a shame this country's so narrow-minded." Josh stared reflectively at the other end of the kitchen, where Fig was crunching the dry cat biscuits. "He sounds like a cow chewing through cornstalks."

Jane looked amused. "You surprise me. I didn't know native New Yorkers knew about such things. I could eliminate the noise, but the only other thing he likes for breakfast is raw liver that's been put through the food blender."

Josh shuddered visibly.

"I know," she said, nodding. "That's the way I feel about it, too. Poor old Fig just has to struggle along."

"Let's leave him to it." Josh pushed back his chair. "Should we do something about these dishes?"

"I inherited Madame Trimpani's daily woman along with Fig. She'll take care of them," Jane said, leading the way out to the hallway.

He stopped there to peer down at her, an uneasy expression on his face. "Seriously, shouldn't you go back to bed for a while?"

She mocked him gently. "Seriously, Mr. Blake—I feel fine. I also have a job to do."

"Forget about that for now. If you aren't going to lie around looking pale and interesting" —he grinned at her increase of color—"we might go down to the hospital and call on Forcada. I could take these pages of script"—he patted the bulge in his hip pocket—"and see if it means anything special. Of course, Nolan may have already been on that route."

"Well, we could try," she murmured. "I wonder if we should tell Lieutenant Nolan about last night?"

"Probably. We can take care of that after we see Emilio."

"All right." Jane was suddenly appalled at the ease with which she was deferring all the important decisions to him. "But I do have a job and I'd better ask permission before I start roaming around the city."

"Permission granted," he said autocratically. "I'll call in from home when I shave and change. Now, I'd better get going before I completely shatter your reputation."

"This is one time when Manhattan anonymity will

come in handy," she said, watching him shrug into a light-colored raincoat. "Uncle Fred won't say anything and I'm sure he'll give the word to Tom, so there's no need to worry."

At that moment, they could hear the elevator door opening outside in the vestibule and the sound of a woman's voice seeped through Madame's bright red door.

"I'm really not surprised to run into you here visiting your patient, Mark, dear," came the familiar, brittle tones. "I told Josh on the way home that Miss Chapin was probably depressed after being ill. I thought the least I could do was stop by and cheer her up."

"Damnation! That's Ellen's voice," Josh said, appalled.

"Just what we needed," Jane replied, trying to suppress a groan. Receiving Ellen Barton would have been a formidable task at any time. To be caught wearing a rumpled flannel nightgown and quilted robe made it even worse than usual. Jane was wondering if she could make a lightning change when she heard Mark's voice as he knocked on the door.

"Jane, can you hear me? I have some company for you."

She grimaced at that, even though she knew he was trying to warn her. Then she turned to Josh and whispered, "Now, what? I've run out of ideas."

"Isn't there a service stair by the back door?" His lips barely moved as he kept his voice low.

"Yes, but I'm not dressed. I can't escape that way."

"Not you—" For an instant he looked as if he was going to break out laughing. Then he controlled himself with an effort. "I meant me," he whispered. "I'll let myself out the back door while you're letting them in the front one. Get rid of them as fast as you can. I'll be back to pick you up in about an hour, but this time, I'll phone from the lobby. Breakfast with you is more crowded than a presidential press conference."

"You know, I think you're right."

He gave her fingers a sympathetic squeeze and disappeared into the kitchen. Jane moved to the front door at the same pace, taking care as she opened it to pull it back all the way so that the kitchen would be momentarily hidden. "Mark," she said brightly, and then she managed an amazed and delighted smile. "Miss Barton—what a surprise!"

"Ellen, please," the other insisted. "I hope this isn't too early to come calling?"

"Can't be," Mark answered for her firmly. "I smell coffee." He caught Jane by the arm when she would have led them on into the living room. "Hey, what happened to your head?"

"I'll tell you later." She clung to her smile as she went on, "I never discuss symptoms standing in the hallway. Why don't you both come on into the kitchen and we can talk there. The coffee's already made and there are even some sweet rolls."

"It sounds good to me," Mark replied. "Ellen?"

"Well, if it isn't any bother. Are you sure we didn't get you out of bed?" she asked Jane after assessing her appearance and obviously concluding that could be the only excuse.

"No, I've been up for ages and I've all sorts of exciting things to report," Jane said, deciding a simple housebreaking would be the best explanation. She started leading them toward the kitchen and then stopped abruptly, remembering the breakfast dishes still on the table. "On the other hand," she said firmly, "we'd be more comfortable sitting here in the living room." And I can save what's left of my reputation, she decided silently.

The forty-five minutes that followed was a testimonial to surface courtesy and conversation. Jane managed to serve coffee, give a capsule version of her midnight housebreaker, satisfy Mark's professional concern about her physical well-being, and convince Ellen that spreading good-will among the sick was just short of joining holy orders. Ellen was so delighted that she suggested lunch and Jane had to admit another appointment.

Mark looked disapproving at that, but Ellen wasn't disposed to linger after asking prettily if there wasn't anything else she could do?

Jane charitably resisted the urge to mention several things Ellen could do and helped her find a missing glove so she could be on the way. Mark was a little harder to uproot until Ellen reminded him that since they were both heading for Continental, they might as well share a cab.

Jane closed the door behind them and spared a few seconds to lean against it, feeling she'd aged five years in the time they were there, trying to skirt around conversational pitfalls.

On the way to the bathroom and a hasty shower, she decided that her greatest triumph was letting Ellen ramble on about Josh Blake. The other woman had made sure that Jane understood how long their families had known each other and what a marvelous friendship existed between her and "dear Josh."

Since "dear Josh" had spent the night on the davenport they were occupying at that moment, Jane had hardly minded the dialogue at all. And later, when she was hastily donning a teal-blue linen dress that just happened to be one of the most flattering things in her wardrobe, she had time to reflect that Josh Blake hadn't appeared enchanted when his old "family friend" had arrived.

The lobby buzzer sounded and Jane lingered for a final

glance in the mirror to check her appearance before heading for the elevator. She might be doing all right in the competition, but it was nice to know that even Ellen couldn't have found fault with the way she looked just then.

Josh, too, looked like a new person as he stood waiting in the lobby of the building. The wrinkled flannels had been exchanged for a lightweight gray suit, and he was wearing a tattersall check shirt and solid-color tie that complemented it nicely.

He peered into the elevator behind her. "You are alone, I trust. No traffic managers hiding behind the door or doctors waiting at the curb?"

"Quite alone, thanks. What about you? No blonde chaperones this time? The last I heard, Miss Barton was planning to drop in on you before lunch—after she'd taken her father's briefcase to him."

"Really." He took her elbow and marched her to a waiting cab without saying anything more.

Men! she thought furiously, and settled in a far corner of the taxi, watching him give the driver the name of the hospital.

Josh settled back in his own corner and surveyed her calmly once they got underway. "You did a good job hiding the lump on your noggin with that hairstyle. It's not quite your type but it serves the purpose. The hairstyle, I mean," he added, straight-faced.

"How do you know what my type is?" Her annoyance showed more than she intended. So much for her attempt to smooth casual waves into a modified chignon.

He refused to be drawn. "Sophisticated hairdos call for sultry brunettes or peroxide blondes. There's too much red in that sandy hair of yours for a sleek disguise." He grinned at her expression. "If you get much madder, that smooth coiffure will be standing on end. I don't know when I've seen a woman rise to a snide comment so fast. You're in the ring before the bell sounds."

"I've never had it happen before. It must be the peculiar effect you have on women," she said, recovering her poise.

"I think I've goofed again." He turned up the collar on his jacket and pretended to shiver. "The cold war's on. I can feel it."

She glanced at him and had to smile. It was unbelievable how full of devilment those brown eyes of his could be when he chose. At other times, his dispassionate appraisal could strip a woman of her dignity and smash her defenses before she even knew what was happening.

Josh saw her smile slowly fade and felt a pang of conscience as he remembered what she'd recently been through. "Don't look at me like that," he said roughly. "I promise to cut out the teasing if you'll reinstate our truce. We were doing so well—I'd hate to start ducking again."

"Honestly . . ." She searched for words and then had to shake her head. "You're terrible."

"Exactly what my mother used to say," he commented calmly.

"Now you make me feel worse than ever. I probably should be apologizing, too."

"Why?" He sounded sincerely surprised. "There's nothing wrong with your manners. Considering the morning you've had, they're downright remarkable." He hesitated, as if considering his words, before going on to ask, "Is it a habit of yours to entertain quite so many men for breakfast?"

"I like the way you put that," she replied, her eyes dancing. "You sound like a census-taker. But if you're really curious—the answer is no. Uncle Fred comes quite often, and if Tom is riding to work with him, he tags along. Mark just decided he wanted a cup of coffee."

"Oh, sure," Josh muttered without conviction. "You left one out, though."

She smoothed her hair back in an effort to hide her confusion. "Well, you don't belong with the rest. Incidentally, I haven't really thanked you for showing up last night. I don't know what I'd have done without you."

"Now that's as neat a red herring as I've heard since I've come to town," he said approvingly. "You're wasting your time in International. Continental should use you in Public Relations."

"If you keep on that way, I'll think *you* have a concussion as well as Emilio. At least, you've come to the right place," she said as the cab drew up to the curb in front of the hospital entrance. A frown creased her forehead as a sudden thought occurred to her. "Will the security guards even let us in to see him?"

"I've cleared this visit," he said after he'd paid the driver and urged her up the steps of the building. "Forcada's in room seven sixteen. Lieutenant Nolan will probably join us there a little later. He was extremely interested when I reported on the state of your apartment last night." An elevator door opened in front of them and he motioned for her to precede him.

"So you did get in touch with him," she said, watching him push the button for the seventh floor. "Was he annoyed that we waited so long?"

Josh was amused by the way she'd unconsciously used the plural pronoun, but he didn't mention it. "It's hard to tell. Nolan must be a good poker player. Here we are," he added, motioning her out onto the seventh floor and checking the number on the nearest door. "Seven ten, seven twelve—it must be down here to the left." Their footsteps echoed in the waxed linoleum corridor, where a busy nurse's station could be seen at the end of the hallway. "This is it," Josh said, halfway down. "Seven sixteen." He pushed open the heavy metal door, leading the way into a spacious if austerely furnished hospital room.

A calm, efficient-looking nurse who appeared to be in her late thirties rose from a chair by the bedside as they entered.

"Good morning," Josh said. "My name is Blake and this is Miss Chapin."

"Lieutenant Nolan said you'd be along," the woman replied in a low voice. "Mr. Forcada has just dozed off."

"Dozed—hell!" The long figure under the white hospital bed covers spoke irritably. "I'm just trying to get a little rest after having my face washed in the middle of the night and being served breakfast before dawn."

"You'll find Mr. Forcada is feeling much stronger," the nurse told them drily. "I'll be outside if you want me for anything." She walked stiffly out of the room.

"All starch and vinegar," Forcada growled. "She's not my type."

Jane smiled. "You really can't expect nurses to wear a rose in their teeth, you know."

"Very funny, *rojita*," Emilio snarled. "That one"—he pointed derisively toward the door—"disapproves of any living breathing being who originates south of Teaneck, New Jersey."

"Now, Emilio," Jane soothed, "you're imagining things again."

"Imagining . . . oh no." Forcada tried to sit up straighter. "Raise this accursed bed a little, will you? That's better. I think that police lieutenant is the one who put her here."

Privately Josh agreed with him, but it was hardly the

time to acknowledge it. "At the rate you're improving, Forcada, you'll be out of here this week."

"So my wife tells me," the South American said somewhat grimly.

Jane settled in a comfortable chair by the bedside. "Has your wife been with you much of the time?"

"Practically twenty-four hours a day," Forcada told them. "Naturally, this has been embarrassing when Anita has wanted to visit."

"Naturally," Jane said.

Forcada's swarthy cheeks flushed unbecomingly. "I am hoping, *rojita,* that you can explain this situation to Anita when you get back to Continental. My wife has suddenly become very devoted and is loathe to . . ." He gestured in a way that belied translation.

"Give you up?" Josh queried, deciding to ignore the gesture.

"Exactly." Forcada sounded resigned.

"Perhaps it's just as well," Jane put in.

Emilio shifted his bandaged head on the pillow. "Just now, it doesn't matter to me. I am much more interested in discovering who put me in this damnable hospital."

So much for romance, Jane concluded. She tried to hide her amusement as she thought how Anita Warren would have hated that casual verbal brush-off. It was obvious that she'd never seen Emilio in the role of a South American husband who would faithfully adhere to the marriage convention.

Or was it that Emilio welcomed this simple answer to his domestic triangle after his earlier transgressions? It was a familiar pattern and certainly not restricted to erring South American husbands. Jane's lips quirked still more. Trust Emilio to extract all the benefits from an awkward situation. By the time his head healed, Anita would have gone on to more rewarding pastures and faithful Señora Forcada would be convinced that her spouse's lapse was only momentary.

"We're sort of here under false pretenses," Josh announced when the silence would have lengthened. He came over to sit in a straight chair that was by the foot of the bed near Jane. "Actually we could use more information on what happened to you the other day."

Forcada groaned and made a face. "Not more questions! Nolan has given me no peace on that score. *Madre de Dios!* If I knew anything, I'd sound off to anybody. All I remember is that I was timing some music—a tango, I think—wondering if it fitted the script. You know, a proper bridge for the dialogue. The next thing, I wake up here."

Josh nodded and pulled the script sheets from his pocket. "I was afraid that's what you'd say. Maybe you can at least show us what part of the script you were on when it happened."

"Oh, all right," Forcada grumbled. "*Rojita,* hand me my glasses, will you?"

"Has the doctor said it's all right for you . . ."

"I'm not planning to read a novel," Emilio said irritably, "but if you want me to see the script, let alone read it, you'd better give me those glasses."

Jane's glance met Josh's briefly and she gave an imperceptible shrug. "I don't imagine it will matter for a few minutes."

Forcada adjusted the black-rimmed glasses over his beaklike nose with an air of triumph. "Ah! Now, then, where was I?" He rifled through the flimsy script sheets impatiently. "Let's see, I'd passed through the Chocano, the Reyes—it seems to me I was going to bring the music up for the second stanza of the Lugones." His voice stopped abruptly. "What's this doing in here?"

"What do you mean?" Josh stood up.

"This one." Forcada shook a piece of paper. "This isn't mine. I never saw it before."

"What is it?" Jane scarcely breathed the words.

Josh grimaced with annoyance as he recognized the selection. "The one that starts 'Send home my harmless heart againe, which no unworthy thought could staine.' " He snapped the script with an impatient finger. "Damn! I should have caught it. John Donne wouldn't normally be included with South American poets."

"John Donne, eh?" Forcada's glasses slipped down on his nose and he peered over them. "Not quite my cup of tea, at least for the audience I have in mind. That's a funny thing to leave around, though."

"Couldn't you have picked up that sheet by mistake?" Jane asked.

"Certainly not. I was the only one with a poetry script in the entire section. I would have noticed it before if it had been shoved in my desk." Forcada removed the glasses and Jane leaned over to take them from him and replace them on the metal table.

"Then you believe it must have been added deliberately to your pile of script in the timing room?" Josh asked.

"What else can I think?" Forcada rubbed a hand over his cheek irritably. "I don't see why they picked on me, though." His smile was sardonic. "The only person who might have felt tempted to hit me over the head was my wife, and she has a solid alibi since she was a thousand miles away at the time. After Anita gets the news about our future, she'll probably feel like giving me another lump."

Josh walked over to the window and stood staring out.

"I wouldn't worry too much about that. Miss Warren looks as if she would be able to take most anything in stride."

"No—you have the wrong idea there. Anita may have been a little too—generous—in the past, but she's been faithful to me," Emilio insisted.

The calm-looking nurse who was on duty reappeared, just in time to keep the sudden silence from becoming awkward. "Lieutenant Nolan phoned to say that he's been delayed, Mr. Blake, but he'll be in touch with you later at your office."

"I see." Josh looked uncertainly at Forcada and then across to Jane. "In that case, we'd better be on our way. Can you think of anything else?"

"Not really," she said. "I'll come back another time, Emilio. Are there any messsages you'd like me to give to the maestro or Horrie?"

"You might tell Horrie that I'm going to need one of his production staff when I get this poetry program going. He'll probably make a big thing out of it, so it needs a little advance planning. Tell him to check with Tom Carmichael about the time slot. I hope young Tomás can tear himself away from his other activities long enough to get down to business."

"I'm sure Tom doesn't mean to let his college work interfere with his job," she said.

"That isn't what I had in mind." Emilio moved restlessly on his hospital bed. "Never mind. Now that things have changed, it doesn't matter anyway."

"What do you mean by that?" Josh wanted to know.

"I'm sorry, Mr. Blake," the nurse moved up to Forcada's bedside, "but I think the patient definitely needs to rest now. The doctor didn't agree to such a long visiting period."

"Very well." Josh's tone was preoccupied. "Come on, Jane. Thanks Emilio, we'll be in touch."

"Sure . . . sure." Forcada sighed. "Sorry I couldn't help you. Nurse, will you shift this pillow for—"

The closing of the heavy hospital door cut off his words in mid-sentence.

Jane stood outside in the corridor and glanced up at Josh's tall form beside her. "Whither away?" she asked.

He thought for a moment before taking her elbow to direct her toward the elevator. "It's time for coffee, but let's have it uptown."

Her steps slowed. "Good heavens, what excuse can I give for showing up at work in the middle of the day?"

"Don't worry. I'll take care of it."

Again she found herself resenting his decisiveness, and her voice was cool. "Do you always appoint yourself judge and jury for your employees?"

"Not always." He nodded toward the opening elevator door and waited until they were inside before adding, "Just for the frail females who need a little guidance."

She preserved a seething silence until they were out of the elevator and finally on the front steps of the building. Then the words burst out. "What an idiotic description of a woman!" she sputtered. "Frail females went out with the hatpin, Mr. Blake. You're not only living in the wrong part of the world—you're in the wrong century, as well! And just because you're a big wheel at Continental doesn't mean that you're going to have any influence on me."

He cut in when she paused for breath. "If you don't simmer down, you're going to have a stroke as well as the remnants of a concussion." He went on, mimicking her formality with some sarcasm, "I just meant that you weren't in condition to go jogging or sign up for the marathon. At least today," he added, leaning over to open the door of an empty cab at the curb. "Tomorrow you can go back to tossing the caber and pumping iron."

She didn't deign to reply, knowing if she did that he would get the better of it again. The safest thing was to remain silent and try to look calm and dignified, which was almost as difficult as some of the alternatives he'd mentioned.

The only interruption came when Josh asked the driver to stop at a bookstore on the way uptown. Jane prudently remained in the waiting cab and when Josh emerged from the shop a few minutes later carrying a small parcel, she managed to contain her curiosity.

It wasn't until the taxi was paid off and they were seated at a table in a smart Fifth Avenue coffee shop that Josh addressed her directly.

"I suppose I'd better be the one to break this stony silence." He smiled slightly. "Although I'm hanged if I know whether it was all my fault. But since you're still under the weather and unable to fight back with full strength, it's the least I can do. Besides"—he paused to let the waitress deposit hot cinnamon rolls and coffee on the table in front of them—"if I don't, you probably won't speak to me for the rest of the month."

"I don't see why that should matter." She shook her head as he offered cream and sugar.

"I'm not sure myself, but it seems to." He stirred his coffee reflectively. "We've had so many 'border incidents' that it's a wonder we're not engaged in a full-scale war."

She sighed and gave him a slightly shamefaced smile. "It's just as well we're not. I have an idea who would win. You always make me feel like a general who has the right maps but the wrong battlefield."

"Now you're pandering to my ego—and that's as it

should be," he replied solemnly. "Lord knows what you can accomplish on that tack."

Her smile widened. "My only objective right now is to finish this cinnamon roll and have a second cup of coffee. The one we had at the apartment was a long time ago."

"Dig in. If you stay with such exemplary behavior, I may even let you have a second helping."

The contented silence reigned between them until the waitress came around to refill their coffee cups.

Jane waited until she'd gone again before saying, "You're right about my having a concussion. I must be out of my mind—eating that huge roll. There were enough calories in it to last a week."

His glance was appraisingly thorough. "You don't have to worry."

"Famous last words," she sighed, leaning back in her chair. "You know, I have a sneaky feeling that you didn't come in here just to ply me with extra calories."

"You're right. It would be nice to relax and close our eyes to everything that's happened, but after last night, I don't think we'd better."

"It seems unreal in the light of day. Perhaps there was no connection between the two incidents. You know how high the petty crime rate is in Manhattan."

"Breaking and entering isn't exactly petty crime. Besides, it's stretching the arm of coincidence pretty far." Josh shoved his empty coffee cup aside to rest his elbow on the table. "If your intruder last night had just walked off with the family jewels, it would be more logical. Instead, he thoroughly ransacked the place—for no apparent reason."

"He probably looked in my jewel box and lost his temper."

Josh chuckled. "Or maybe he took one look at the decor in the living room and went berserk. It's possible but not very probable." His expression sobered as he went on. "Lieutenant Nolan didn't think much of the coincidence angle either."

"I'd like to have talked to him."

"He'll probably catch up with us at work later." Josh leaned down and retrieved the parcel he'd brought with him. After tearing off the wrapping, he held up a thin book. "I thought this might be helpful after Forcada's disclosure. Strictly a hunch on my part."

She reached across the table for it and flipped through the pages. "Poems by John Donne. This time, you'll have to translate. I'm out of my field."

Josh's expression turned rueful. "What makes you think I'm in mine? My college literature class is way behind me, but that poem in Emilio's script somehow rang a bell. I thought the other verses might clue us in."

Jane bit her lip, uncomprehending. "I must be thicker than usual. Clue us in to what?"

"The reason why the poem was included in the script at all. Emilio swears it wasn't his idea." Josh reached for the book. "Anyhow, it's the only lead."

"I hope you're right." She hunched over the table to watch him leaf through the pages, completely intent on his task. "Other than the South American poets, I just have a distant acquaintance with Christina Rossetti and Robert Browning."

"A true romantic in your tastes," Josh commented absently, not looking up. "I hope to god that poem is in this anthology. I didn't want to waste time in the bookstore looking for it."

"Because you had a cab waiting . . ." she teased.

"With an unhappy woman as the other fare," he finished solemnly. "I was afraid that if I didn't get back in a hurry, she'd leave me stranded." Josh kept his head bent over the book. "Dammit, if I could remember the first line of the poem I could check the index. Wait a minute—here it is."

Jane sobered instantly. "For heaven's sake, read it."

"It's called 'The Message.' There are three verses," he said, scanning the page. "The one in the script is the second one. Listen to the final one, though," he added triumphantly.

When thou
Art in anguish
And dost languish
  For some one
  That will none
Or prove as false as thou art now.

Josh's voice trailed off on the final word and he raised his glance to meet hers. "How about that?"

Jane took a deep breath and then decided to tell the truth. "Frankly, Ogden Nash is more my type over the long run. Mr. Donne is too bitter for me."

"Exactly. It's completely different from the rest of the stuff that Emilio had included."

"Which means what?"

Josh was studying the poem again. "It could be an accusation—maybe against Forcada. 'As false as thou art now' is really throwing down the gauntlet."

"Emilio is the most likely body," she said, picking up a spoon from the table and fiddling with it aimlessly. "I wonder, though. That meaning could have been aimed at someone else—and Emilio just got caught in the middle."

Josh rubbed his chin as he thought about it and then shook his head. "That theory won't hold water. Emilio was in the timing room minding his own business. Somebody went into the room deliberately, taking a weapon along, and committed the assault."

"I suppose you're right." From her tone, it was obvious she wasn't convinced.

Josh put the book on the table between them. "You sound just like some jury foremen I've known. Where do we differ?"

"I don't quite know how to explain." She bit her lip again nervously, and then her words came out in a rush. "Honestly, I don't know why I even offer an opinion. I've never once suspected the guilty person when I watch a mystery on television."

"Stop being such a shy violet," he told her irritably, "and get on with it. Do you imagine I'm such an autocrat that I can't stand to have a few holes punched in a half-baked theory?"

His tone made color surge to her cheeks. "Of course not," she snapped back. "Only I don't really have a valid opinion. That's why I feel silly trying to be logical."

"Let me be the judge. There's no need to dither like some featherbrain. If it helps your ego, I've seen you display a commendable amount of gray matter at times." His glance lingered on her stormy features. "Although now isn't one of the times."

"Thank you very much." She lined up the spoon to a careful forty-five degree angle to her water glass. It took some time, and when she spoke again, her fury had subsided. "You're losing your temper again," she told him solemnly. "I imagine it's because you missed so much sleep last night. My landlady's davenport isn't the greatest."

Josh's lips quirked, almost unwillingly. "At least that

gives me a logical excuse. Where were we before this last skirmish?"

"I was about to say that premeditation doesn't fit in with my interpretation of Donne's poem. But even if it applied to Emilio, it couldn't have anything to do with the intruder in my apartment." She tapped a shapely finger on the book between them. "That line in the poem about languishing for someone and hoping they won't prove false doesn't help, either. In the first place, nobody's ever languished for me and I've never been part of a triangle in my life. If this poetry figures in the scheme of things, my prowler must have picked the wrong floor."

"Possibly. Although as one of the four men who appeared in your apartment this morning, I can testify that you're not pining for masculine companionship."

"That's a lot of malarky. Now if Emilio made a habit of appearing at my front door . . ."

"Does he?" For the life of him, Josh couldn't choke back the brusque question.

"Emilio!" Jane was incredulous. "Why, he's never been to my apartment in his life. I'm not his type at all." A small smile played around her lips. "You're sure that you didn't fall off the couch last night on your head?"

"Probably it's the onset of blood poisoning brought on by that cat of yours," Josh said lightly. "I may sue, after all."

He was determined not to show the unutterable relief he felt at Jane's spirited denial. For a moment, he had a niggling suspicion of why he felt so strongly and then cleared his throat self-consciously, aware that it wasn't the moment to probe further along those lines.

Jane did her best to appear unconcerned, despite his searching stare. Her flushed countenance showed that she was neither immune to his regard nor succeeding very well in suppressing her reactions. Even a stranger would have noticed the shy response in her glance, the tempting curve of her lips, and the breathless, husky quality of her voice.

She, too, wished there were more time to analyze the feeling that was raising her pulse rate so alarmingly. The malady was admittedly familiar, but she had never experienced it before to such a degree. With almost fatalistic certainty, she knew that she would never feel quite the same way again.

The same instinct cautioned that she was letting herself in for real trouble. When a woman was dealing with a man like Josh Blake, there was little hope for the uncomplicated "happy ever after" ending. And if a gorgeous creature like Ellen Barton hadn't lined him up for the matrimonial stakes, there wasn't any chance for ordinary women. Especially one with freckles on her nose—who made him lose his temper every five minutes.

There was the additional possibility that Ellen was telling the truth about a mythical engagement announcement being only hours away. On her visit that morning, she'd chronicled the long friendship between the Bartons and the Blakes, intimating that an official notice would appear in practically the next edition of the society page.

Jane knew that Josh was the type of man who'd be faithful to his fiancée if he had one. But was he really going to claim that particular one? She sighed softly, fearing there must be some basis to Ellen's words because no woman would risk certain humiliation otherwise.

That conclusion made Jane decide to put her own dream away. Only now, she'd wrap it in a strong, protective coating because it was a fragile flight of fancy that couldn't stand up to the heartbreaking reality of life.

Josh watched the impassive mask cover Jane's face as a

thin fog would obscure the sun and he narrowed his eyes in concern.

"Sure you won't have another cup of coffee?" he asked, merely for something to say.

"Quite sure, thanks." She started making the motions that precede all feminine leave-taking. "Sorry I couldn't be of more help. This was one time when that Spanish proverb about 'four eyes seeing more than two' didn't apply."

"Don't forget, those two eyes of yours were closed most of the time last night," he replied. "Come on, I'll pay the check and then we'll walk to work if you feel up to it."

"Of course." She kept her voice carefully impersonal. "The fresh air will feel good. It might even help clear the cobwebs. Otherwise, when Lieutenant Nolan comes asking questions, he'll be completely disgusted with me."

She had plenty of time on their walk back to Continental to mentally rehearse her next lines and when they reached the main entrance, she put out her hand in a formal gesture of thanks. "In case I don't get a chance later, I want to let you know how much I've appreciated your thoughtfulness."

He took her hand and stared at her, plainly puzzled. "You sound as if you're saying farewell forever."

"I didn't mean it that way," she said, wishing to heaven that it was true. The prospect of being on hand to watch Ellen's eventual triumph wasn't pleasant. She managed a thin smile as she went on, "It's just that you're busy and Mark said something about transferring me to the domestic side of the network. Oh, before I forget—I gave Miss Barton my good wishes but I wanted to congratulate you, as well."

"What in the devil are you talking about?"

"Your impending engagement. Ellen said you weren't

announcing it officially for a little while, but since I'll be leaving shortly, she didn't mind my knowing."

There was a pause while she thought, Dear god, let him deny it. Let him say it isn't true.

Unfortunately, the embarrassing moment dragged on while each studiously avoided the other's eyes. A muscle tightened in Josh's jaw, but his only other reaction was to look profoundly ill-at-ease.

Jane managed to break the silence first. "So that's that," she said in a bright and brittle tone. "We probably won't have time for any real get-together after this, but I hope I'll see you around."

"I wouldn't count on it," Josh said with cold finality. "I have to leave tomorrow for a business trip to Washington, D.C. and Los Angeles."

"I see." The only way Jane could avoid his steely glance was to center her attention on the zipper of her purse. She opened it and rummaged for a handkerchief she didn't need, saying, "Then I'll probably be on my way by the time you get back."

Her eyes filled with tears and she was turning blindly toward the building when Josh put out a detaining hand. He pulled her back against him so forcefully that she let out a surprised gasp as she collided with his solid length.

"It's too damned bad that I couldn't have knocked some sense into you last night," he grated out. "On the other hand, I'm not married yet." He tilted her chin ruthlessly and bent his head to cover her parted lips with his in a fierce, possessive kiss that made even some blasé New Yorkers pause to admire the spectacle before continuing along the sidewalk.

When Josh released Jane a half-minute later, it was fortunate that she was next to the building facade, because if she couldn't have leaned against the solid marble, she would simply have dissolved on the sidewalk like a tar strip in the hot sun.

Josh didn't stick around to see her reaction. She was barely able to focus on his tall form as he strode through the doorway without a single backward glance. Fortunately he was out of sight when the tears started rolling down her cheeks.

# Chapter Eight

ⅹ ⅹ ⅹ

Considering it was late morning, the part of International near Jane's desk was surprisingly quiet and deserted when she arrived.

She had carefully detoured by the downstairs ladies lounge to powder away any evidence of her recent tears, but she was glad that she didn't have to put her wan and unhappy face to the test right away.

"¡Hola, rojita! ¿Qué tal?"

Jane whirled to see Horrie lounging in the doorway behind her. "Oh, lord, you startled me," she gasped. "You'll have to start stomping down the hall when you come around. Where is everybody, by the way?"

The production chief frowned. "When zere are two uff us," he said in a terrible Hungarian accent, "vye do ve need anvone ulse?"

"Right now, I don't need anybody," she said, hoping

he'd take the hint. "There's a pack of work to catch up on before I can goof off."

"Let me help you," he said eagerly.

"In which category?"

"It doesn't matter—I'm pretty talented in both."

She slammed a desk drawer shut. "You'll never convince me with that Lothario routine. Why you'd be shocked if I even flirted with you." Her voice was more caustic than she knew. While one part of her mind carried on the conversation with Horrie, she was still reliving that bitter farewell embrace on the sidewalk. By then, anger at Josh's inexplicable behavior was her only defense against the overwhelming desire that his kiss had triggered.

Her sarcasm didn't even register with the production chief. "That's what you think," he said, leering unconvincingly. "Try me. Oh, all right," he went on when her lips tightened, "if you insist on working—I can give you a roll call of the whole place. Most of my people are over on the domestic side listening to a rehearsal of a pilot program. The foreign sections are still mainly off-duty and Madge is on some errand uptown for Papa Fred. Tomás is busy with his network counterpart threshing out clearance for the new season's schedule, and from some elevated perch"—Horrie's arms went up in an extravagant gesture—"our assistant boss is undoubtedly watching over us benignly."

Jane was still for a moment and then she turned to stare at Horrie curiously. "You don't like Josh, do you?"

Horrie's cherubic features sobered. "Mine is not to like or dislike, *chiquita*. The man is here to wield a big axe. My head will be one of the first to roll."

Her eyes narrowed. "What makes you think so?"

"I've been getting in too deep on the political front. If I stay, the network will be after me. If I try to pull out"—he shrugged—"that's unhealthy, too. Some of the membership play rough."

"Do you think that's what happened to Emilio?"

"Of course. Unless he was attacked by a star-crossed lover, and that's hardly likely. Anita doesn't inspire that kind of devotion." Horrie jingled some coins in his pocket absently. "The other possibility is that his wife got tired of the hole and corner affair and did the dastardly deed herself."

"That would have been difficult. Emilio says she was a thousand miles away."

"Maybe her papa put out a contract." When Jane just looked at him, Horrie shrugged. "I guess I'm jealous of her alibi. That Lieutenant Nolan is too eager for my way of thinking. His constant poking around is getting on my nerves."

"Probably the only thing that's wrong with you is a case of 'expectant fatheritis.' " Her tone softened. "How much sleep did you get last night?"

"Not enough. My wife had insomnia again, so we spent part of the night playing double solitaire."

"You're not going to be much good to that baby if you're completely exhausted when it arrives."

"Watch your grammar, *rojita*. The word is 'he'—not 'it.' "

"You can't fool me. You'll be just as thrilled if it's a girl," she replied. "Seriously though, why don't you try taking it a little easier."

He beamed. "That's what I was hoping you'd say. Especially since I planned to borrow the couch again for a short nap."

"Be my guest. At this rate, we'll never get it out of the department, but I guess it really doesn't matter. Put a

145

blanket over you so you'll look suitably infirm in case anybody walks by."

"It's too hot. Besides, the only person who'd matter is
Josh Blake, and if he appears, I start shaking anyhow."

"In that case, tell him you're suffering from occupa-
tional fatigue. You might even get a few days off. Now lie
down and get some rest."

Jane started back toward her desk and then recalled
that Fred Hall would probably be expecting to see her.
The quizzical look he had on his face during his visit to
the apartment showed that he was taking his job as a sub-
stitute parent seriously. His manner had indicated that
he'd go along with the story then but that he'd expect a
more satisfactory explanation for Josh's presence in short
order.

Knowing her honorary uncle's dogged determination,
Jane decided it would be easiest just to tell him the whole
story. If she included her plan of a transfer out of International to the domestic side of the network, he'd realize
that Josh's overnight aid had been just that. Nothing
more.

She turned resolutely toward Fred Hall's office, noticing
as she walked down the hallway and passed Josh's quarters that his door was closed and the room was dark. She
wondered if he was remembering their stormy parting at
that moment, just as she was. Probably not. Not with Ellen close by to soothe his ruffled feelings.

As she marched on toward the executive office, she
noted that Tom's desk was empty as well as Madge's
nearby. Strange that they'd both be gone at the same
time, she thought, since the house rule was that they covered for each other.

Everything was out of sync in the world, she decided,
wishing that she'd read the headlines in the morning pa-

per so she would have had somewhere to place all the blame. She rapped gently on Fred Hall's door and when there was no response, she knocked again. "Damn," she murmured in frustration, as silence reigned. Obviously she was going to strike out in another league.

She had a baffled look as she stared around her at the deserted desks. If appearances were anything to go by, it might be a holiday rather than an ordinary day of the week. Of course, Uncle Fred could have gone out to a meeting, but it was strange that Horrie hadn't mentioned it. She knocked on the door again firmly and then reached for the knob, finding it turned easily under her fingers.

She took a cautious step inside the executive office, hovering on the threshold before going further. The place loomed emptily in front of her and she gave herself a mental shake. It was as if she'd been waiting for a fire-cracker to explode and suddenly realized that the fuse had gone out. With another casual look around, she turned to leave.

The sound of a thin moan stopped her. It was so faint that she almost attributed it to her overactive imagination. Even so, she would still have marched out, closing the door firmly behind her, but for the stronger sense of fore-boding which stayed her hand on the knob. She turned and walked over to the big mahogany desk in the corner of the room.

A pile of script was untidily strewn about on the sur-face, with an opened telephone reminder book turned face down beside it. Alongside was a well-worn, leather-cov-ered volume with a faded gold title: JOHN DONNE.

Josh's book, Jane thought immediately, and then put a brake on her rampaging imagination. Of course it wasn't the same book that Josh had shown her. Her worried gaze moved on and stopped in horror as it lit on the motionless figure of Frederick Hall, lying crumpled on the rug behind the desk.

She drew a stricken breath and then flung herself to her knees beside him, her fingers feeling automatically for a pulse in his outflung wrist. As she tried desperately to count the faint beat, she was conscious that his sparse gray hair was tousled and his tie askew under the torn collar of his shirt. Blood oozed from a shallow cut on his cheek that went from eyebrow to jawline.

He moaned feebly as she smoothed the thin hair back from his colorless forehead. She frowned as she tried to think of the best thing to do; she'd have to leave him for a moment to get help—that was certain. The fall he'd sustained could have aggravated his chronic heart condition and his age wouldn't help matters. Fortunately the cut on his cheek appeared worse than it actually was. She lingered an instant longer to watch the rise and fall of his chest before turning swiftly to his office door. As she pulled it open, she cannoned into Josh, who grasped her shoulders to keep his balance.

"For pete's sakes, where's the fire?" he growled. "You know better than to come ploughing through doors in this place."

"Oh, stop it," she snapped, cutting him short. "Fred's hurt." She gestured behind her as she went on. "Stay with him while I get more help, and don't let him move whatever you do."

Josh stared, open-mouthed, at her retreating back and then pushed on into Hall's office, automatically closing the door behind him. As he knelt beside the older man and unconsciously caught his hand in a comforting grasp, the division chief opened his eyes and peered up in bewilderment.

"It's all right," Josh said, bending closer. "Just rest easy for a few minutes."

The faded eyes continued to stare at him. Then the older man swallowed with an effort and opened his mouth to speak.

Josh put his head down by the other's lips to hear four feeble, disjointed words. Once Hall whispered them, his eyelids flickered and closed again.

Josh straightened and frowned down at the motionless figure on the rug. He repeated the four words under his breath as he watched the rise and fall of the older man's chest, just as Jane had done earlier. And then suddenly she was back again.

"I was able to reach Mark in his office and he'll be right down." She peered at Hall anxiously. "Has there been any change?"

"He regained consciousness for a second or two and some words came out, but they didn't make sense."

"I don't think that's unusual. What did he say?"

"Just four words—'too much' and 'it's hell.' "

She stared at him, obviously puzzled. "You must be mistaken. That doesn't make any sense at all."

"There's nothing wrong with my hearing, no matter what you think," Josh said definitely.

"I'm sorry, I didn't mean to sound so dogmatic. He probably is just incoherent." Her frown deepened. "I wish I knew what it all meant. At least, his color seems better."

"How do you suppose he got that cut?" Josh asked in a low tone. "It certainly didn't come from hitting the corner of the desk when he fell."

"I know. That leaves only—"

"Our mysterious friend? Could be." He shook his head. "It seems far-fetched, though."

Jane hardly knew whether to weep or laugh. "That's putting it mildly. This whole thing is one big horror story—I wonder if it will ever end."

At that moment, Mark Jamieson hurried into the office carrying his black bag. Josh saw the expression of relief on Jane's face and felt a surge of anger.

My god, he thought, I'd better get out of here before I really make a fool of myself. Aloud, he managed a creditable, "I'll be in my office if you need any extra help."

"Sure thing, Josh," Mark said absently as he pulled a stethoscope from his bag and put it to his ears. He motioned for Jane to unbutton Hall's shirt and bent to the older man's chest, listening intently.

Jane watched his expression anxiously. It was hard to remain impersonal when the memories of Frederick Hall's kindness to her over the years crowded her mind. She continued to watch as Mark finally removed the instrument and put it back in the bag at his side.

"I think he'll do, Janie. Let's take him next door to that old dispensary 'til he comes around properly. Get somebody to shove that couch back in there for some privacy. Afterward, he'll need someone to take care of him at home."

"He lives in a private club uptown. There must be help during the day, and I can take over after work if he needs anyone else."

Jamieson looked at her consideringly. "I don't think you're in any shape for night nursing, my girl. If this keeps up, you'll be in need of a nurse yourself."

"I feel fine." Jane made her voice brisk and impersonal. "Give me a minute to make sure everything's ready next door."

A low moan came from the inert figure at their feet.

"It looks as if he's coming around," Mark said. "You'd better cut along, Janie."

"Right. I won't be long." As she went out past Madge's desk and the traffic corner, she noted that they were still vacant. The secretary and Tom must be taking an extended vacation, she decided. It was too bad—just when she could have used the traffic manager's help in moving that couch.

The door of the old dispensary was tightly closed, and suddenly she recalled that Horrie was resting on the couch in the hall. He wouldn't take kindly to having his siesta so rudely interrupted, but there was no alternative.

"Horrie," she called urgently down the corridor. "Horrie, wake up!"

"Leave him alone, Janie girl," came a rough whisper behind her.

"Oh!" Her voice squeaked in surprise as she whirled to face the figure which moved close to her side. "You! For heavens sake, what do you mean by standing behind the door and almost scaring me to death? You'd better get out of here and help Dr. Jamieson with Uncle Fred."

"I don't think you need my help."

"Will you stop being an idiot." She removed her elbow from the tightening grasp. "And stop hurting me or I'll be black and blue."

"Then stop calling me an idiot. It's the second time you have, you know." There was almost a plaintive tone to the words. "I didn't think you'd ever say that, Janie. Fred called me a fool and Emilio said something worse than that. That's why I had to hurt them, Janie. And now"—his voice was reproachful—"now you've made it so I have to hurt you, too." There was the glitter of steel in the hand at his side. "It's a good thing I took this out of the drawer in the old drug cabinet this morning, but I didn't want to get it bloody."

"You can't mean it!" There was horror in Jane's voice and on her face, as well. "I never dreamed . . ." Her words broke as she continued to stare upward at the ravaged face of Tom Carmichael, who was gripping a narrow, blood-smeared knife in his hand.

"I didn't want to hurt anybody, Janie." His voice was repeating in her ears. "I was glad that you fainted last night before you saw me, but now it's all spoiled again. If I could just have been left alone, none of it would have happened." He looked down at her nervously and then over at Horrie's still figure. "I didn't expect him to be here."

"You haven't hurt Horrie, too!" There was a touch of hysteria in Jane's voice as she started for the quiet figure on the couch, but Carmichael's fingers bit into her arm.

"Not yet." Tom kept his voice low and threatening. "And I won't have to if he keeps on sleeping, but that's one I wouldn't mind running this knife into." He looked down at the blade as if figuring the odds. "Considering some of those rotten political connections he's been supporting, it might be the best thing." Tom's lip curled unpleasantly. "It's a funny thing, Janie girl—once you start this, it's hard to stop. You'd be surprised how easy it comes."

Jane swallowed and tried to hide her fear as she said, "You don't mean that, Tom. Not really." Obviously, he'd suffered some kind of a breakdown, and if she could only persuade him to put down the knife and talk about it, further tragedy might be avoided. "You're just tired," she added. "Let me help you. I'll get—"

"You'll get nobody," he snarled, cutting her off in fury. "No way. I'm not hanging around waiting for that damn police lieutenant to figure out the tune. This is a good time to leave. A good time for both of us," he added, hefting the knife suggestively. "I haven't decided what to do with you. If you behave, we might work something out."

She clutched at his arm. "We can't leave now. You have the wrong idea about all this . . ."

"Wrong, hell!" He shook her off roughly. "There's nothing to be gained by hanging around. Fred's beyond help—he tried to take the knife away from me . . . there was all that blood . . . then he just dropped like a rock." Carmichael's eyes gleamed with panic. "God, I didn't know he'd collapse. Why didn't you ever say that his heart was bad? And why in the hell did you tell him about that poem of Donne's?" His voice rose threateningly. "You're just as lousy as Anita and she's a devil's curse to any man."

Jane held her head in despair. Obviously he was farther gone than she'd feared—talking about curses like a man possessed.

Precisely at that moment, there was a sudden movement on the couch and Horrie Cole sat up, swinging his legs to the floor. "It's like trying to sleep in a sheet metal shop," he complained. "Even home is quieter than this blasted place, *rojita*. Why don't you two pick one of the studios if you have to argue." He stopped rubbing his face long enough to focus on Tom's ominous figure. "What in the hell's going on that you need a knife? If you insist on playing games, pick another spot so I can get some sleep." Horrie bent down to retrieve his pillow but didn't stop complaining. "The minute I close my eyes, you start carrying on like a maniac. . . ."

His word was ill-chosen.

Tom jerked convulsively and started toward him, his

knife raised. "Damn your rotten hide! I'll show you who's the maniac!"

"Tom, stop it!" Jane shrieked, hauling on his upraised arm and forgetting her own safety as she struggled with the enraged man beside her. "Put that knife down!"

"Keep him away from me," Horrie yelled, shrinking back against the leather couch. "He's off his rocker!"

"I can still take care of you," Tom gritted out. He tried to shake free of Jane's grip. "Let go of me or I'll—"

Jane saw the knife blade in front of her face and screamed, putting up her arms to defend herself. At the same moment, Tom slammed his open hand against her throat and sent her flying across the corridor. She hit the opposite wall hard and, in the split second before she crumpled to the floor, saw Josh burst on the scene and start for Tom's crouched figure.

"Josh . . ." she managed to whisper just once before darkness settled down.

It seemed a long time before anything else happened. Then she was dimly aware of being scooped up and put on a softer surface.

"Don't cry, Jane," advised a soothing masculine voice close to her ear. "Open your eyes. Everything's all right now."

She felt something cool on her forehead and her eyelids fluttered. There were two figures nearby and another at her side, she decided. As she focused with difficulty, she discovered it was Mark doing the mysterious things to her head. Fretfully she tried to push his hands away.

"I'm all right." She struggled up on one elbow despite his restraining hand at her shoulder. "What happened to Tom?" A sob formed in her throat. "He didn't mean to hurt me—I know he didn't mean it."

"It's okay, Janie." Mark didn't raise his voice but it stopped her panic effectively. "Josh took care of him."

"He's all right?"

"Carmichael? Oh, yes. He's on his way to a hospital right now. Under restraint, of course."

"No, no." She shook her head vexedly. "I mean Josh. Did he get hurt?"

"I'm fine, Jane." The other tall figure came closer to the couch. "And so is Fred. Mark has him resting on some cushions in his office until he patches you up."

She sank back against the leather couch, aware that her head was throbbing. "Just as soon as I can get rid of this headache, I'll be all right. Won't I, Mark?"

It was fortunate that she didn't see the worried glance that Josh gave Mark Jamieson.

"Of course you will." The doctor's normally crisp voice sounded strangely husky. "In fact, Horrie here was reluctant to give up his couch. He was sure he needed it more than you did."

"That's right, *rojita*." Horrie moved hesitantly closer. "After I watched Josh give Tom a right to the jaw to get that knife away from him, the stuffing went out of my knees. It's a wonder that I didn't need a stretcher, too."

Jane's eyes, already dark with pain, seemed to darken still more as she sorted through his words. "Josh—you didn't hurt him?" she asked, trying to see his face.

"Carmichael will recover," Mark broke in firmly. "By the time his sedation wears off, I doubt if he'll remember much of what happened."

"But if Josh knocked him down . . ."

Horrie bent over her. "What did you expect?" His voice climbed in excitement as he continued. "There you were, lying on the floor like a bundle of wet wash. Josh took one look at you and pulled Tom around to connect with that uppercut. Tom actually bounced when he hit the floor. I've never seen anything like it outside of the ring."

"Tom's head is harder than yours," Jamieson told Jane when he could get a word in. "That's why I'm giving you a shot right now for a nice long rest. Don't try to argue, I won't even listen."

She sighed and let her eyes close, stirring restlessly as alcohol was rubbed on her arm before the slight prick of the hypodermic needle.

"There, now." Mark patted her shoulder when it was over. "Just relax. I have some other things to do."

As if in the distance, she heard a low conversation about an ambulance arriving. It must be for Uncle Fred, she decided, trying to sort through the fog that was descending in her mind. He must have been badly hurt, after all. There was a gentle touch on her hand and her eyes opened slowly.

"Jane, can you hear me?"

She just barely managed to make out Josh's features close to hers. But what a difference from his usual impassive expression! His forehead was creased with worry and he looked as if he hadn't slept for a week. His hand grasped hers tightly. "Listen, darling—you'll have to pay attention. Mark will be back in a minute and boot me out of here."

Jane let her eyelids fall and a dreamy smile came over her pale face. "What a funny drug." The words were thick and slow. "I thought—I thought you said something . . ."

"Jane, listen to me. They're coming for you now."

"Who's coming?" Her question didn't even make sense in her own ears and it was too much of an effort to open her eyes. It was a pity, she thought, that real life couldn't be like a dream.

"Do just what Mark says, darling. I'll see you as soon as I can." The voice came from a great distance that time. Something whisper-light brushed her lips and she sighed painfully. Wouldn't Mark be annoyed if he knew what his sedative had started. She started to smile and stopped abruptly as a wave of pain swept over her. Then, mercifully, the drug took hold and all coherent thought was swept away into the darkness.

# Chapter Nine

### ∾ ∾ ∾

"Home is the sailor—home from the sea," Jane announced a week later as she and Fred Hall stepped into the twelfth-floor hallway and approached Madame Trimpani's ornate door. "And the hunter home from the hill. Although by rights, I should be singing Puccini when I approach this place rather than quoting Stevenson."

"Not if you're counting on me for a duet," the older man said as he put down her overnight case in front of it. "Let me have your key and I'll do the honors."

"Here it is." She handed it over and then reached for her case. "You should have let me carry this. It was marvelous of you to bring me home from the hospital, but you really should be at your place resting."

"That's nonsense. You'll have me turning into an old crock." Hall twisted the key and put his weight against the heavy door. "Here we go. Getting into your apartment is like blasting into a bank vault."

"Well, at least I won't have to struggle with it much longer." She led the way into the hall, putting her purse on the telephone table before catching sight of a dazzling bouquet at one end of the davenport. "Oh, how lovely! I'll bet you put Madge up to that," she told Fred Hall over her shoulder as he closed the door. "It was so nice of her to come in and take care of things while I was gone."

Just then, she noticed a plump black and white form ambling toward them from the living room and she hurried over to lift him in her arms. "Fig! Were you feeling completely neglected?" As she rubbed behind his ears, his front paws kneaded her forearm and a purr rumbled from his chest. Jane surveyed him fondly. "You certainly haven't missed any meals. I hope you thanked your friend Madge for that." She bent to deposit him back on the floor and straightened, saying, "Let me take your topcoat, Uncle Fred, and then let's have some coffee."

His thin face lighted with a smile. "That sounds good. This is like old times. Why don't we have it in the kitchen?"

She hung his coat in the closet and came back, smiling. "The kitchen it is—if you'll promise to just sit and watch. You know what Mark said about your taking it easy for a while."

"You're a fine one to talk," he said, following her to the kitchen and sitting on a chair by the window while she put some water in the kettle to heat. "If we're comparing cases, I'm sure that Mark Jamieson didn't approve of your leaving town this evening."

"Once he heard that I was practically going on a slow freight with stopovers in Montreal and Banff, he didn't mind." She reached in a cupboard for coffee and filled a filter in the glass dripolater. "Besides, I'm feeling fine now. It's just that with all the things I accumulated in

South America, it's more economical to go by train than fly. So I refuse to be treated as an invalid."

"Well, you've certainly had us all worried. That 'no visitors' sign was on your hospital room door longer than I liked."

"A head injury can be tricky," she admitted, putting place mats on the table. "I'm lucky that mine wasn't as bad as they feared. Do you suppose Madge might have left some cream in the refrigerator?"

"Why don't you look?" he suggested drily. "But if you want to change the subject, just say so."

Jane ignored that. "She did remember," she said, her voice muffled as she investigated the refrigerator's innards. "Madge is a positive jewel. I hope you appreciate her."

"If I don't, she reminds me. Speaking of Madge, I should call and leave this number in case she wants to reach me."

"Sorry, you can't." Jane brought a cream pitcher and sugar bowl to the table. "I had the telephone service cut off yesterday. As soon as I knew that I wouldn't be staying in town any longer."

"I see." Hall settled back in his chair to watch her pour the boiling water into the beaker. Immediately, the fragrance of brewing coffee filled the air. "You know, you've never explained this sudden decision to leave. I realize it was a temporary job, but I also know that your father wasn't expecting you home for another month, so you can't use him for an excuse."

"That's true." She brought the coffee beaker to the table and sat down on a chair across from him. "But after all the things that happened, it seemed best this way."

An expression of pain flickered over his thin face. "I can understand your feeling about Tom—although the last report I had from his doctor was encouraging. That's not a valid reason, though. You could have at least waited until Josh got back and then given the usual notice."

She kept her glance resolutely on the coffee she was pouring into his cup. "Help yourself to cream and sugar, won't you."

"Jane, dear . . ." His voice was level but insistent. "You didn't answer my question."

She put the beaker down so suddenly that the steaming coffee almost went over the edge. "I'm sorry, Uncle Fred—but honestly, there's no use going over it all again. My reservations are made. I'm leaving tonight, and that's all there is to it." Absently, she moved the coffee onto a warming tray and sat back in her chair as if all the strength had gone out of her. "Besides, there's no telling when Josh will be back. After he attended that committee meeting in Washington with Mr. Barton, I understood they were joining Ellen and flying on to Los Angeles."

"Jane, my dear, you have the story all wrong, and you know it," Fred Hall reproved. "Probably Josh tried to call himself, but there was no chance of getting past that hospital switchboard—I know that for a fact." When she didn't reply, he went on persuasively, "I heard from Washington that things now look favorable for our appropriation since that committee meeting. Incidentally, Ellen accompanied her father down there."

"Don't be naïve, Uncle Fred." Jane took a sip of coffee and put the cup carefully back in the saucer, giving it undue attention. "It's obvious that where Josh goes, Ellen goes as well. He didn't even bother to deny the engagement announcement she was spreading all over Continental."

"Good heavens, girl, how could he deny anything? For the past week, you've been incarcerated in the hospital and now you're holed up in here with the telephone cut off. Tonight, you'll be taking off again."

"I'm not deliberately avoiding anything," she said, her voice rising with unhappiness. "There's just no use staying around when there's no future to it. You'd never have found out how I felt, if you hadn't caught me in that weak moment at the hospital."

"Dissolving into tears because Ellen went to Washington," he said scathingly. "It never occurred to you, I suppose, that adding two and one does *not* make a cozy twosome."

Jane rubbed her forehead. "All this ridiculous talk has given me a headache."

"Very well, then, we'll change the subject." Fred Hall tactfully refrained from mentioning that the cause of her particular headache wouldn't be erased quite so easily. Instead he let a compassionate glance go over her troubled pale face and said, "You know, Jane, I envy you. Imagine going out to breathe really fresh air in your part of the country instead of riding a hot subway to work."

"It does sound wonderful! You'd better plan your vacation out there this year."

"I'll try." Hall fiddled with the spoon on his saucer as he said in a concerned voice, "By then, Tom's troubles should be resolved one way or the other. In the meantime, I'll have to stay around and see if I can help in any way."

"It's wonderful of you to accept some responsibility. He doesn't have anybody else, does he?"

"Not really. I've been practically a second father to him ever since he's worked for International. I should have noticed that he couldn't cope with a full-time job and college as well."

Jane frowned disbelievingly. "Surely that didn't trigger his attack on poor Emilio?"

"No, dammit." The older man winced as if in pain. "There's no denying that he planned that ahead of time. Otherwise, he wouldn't have taken the weapon and had the poem by John Donne ready to slip in that script."

Jane refilled their coffee cups in the silence that followed his words. Then she asked quietly, "What kind of a weapon did he use?"

"A steel bar from a sound effects cart. Afterward, he washed it off and put it back where it was supposed to be. Thank god he didn't hit Emilio any harder, or there wouldn't be any defense at all."

She nodded. "I understand that even Emilio is recommending leniency. Frankly, I was surprised to hear it."

"Probably because he knows that his own hands aren't too clean. I've found out that Tom and Anita had been 'going together' for some time before Emilio came on the scene."

Jane smiled faintly at Hall's diplomatic phrasing. "I can guess what happened then. Anita saw a chance of better things with Emilio, so she dumped Tom by the wayside."

"Something like that."

"Then that's why he left the Donne there? As a threat?"

Fred Hall nodded. "It was a warning for Emilio to move on. Tom knew that Emilio liked poetry so he thought he was being clever in leaving that selection."

"But Emilio didn't tumble to it—even in the hospital he just told us that the paper wasn't his. I think Tom had grandiose ideas about the whole thing. John Donne's symbolism was beyond me—and apparently Emilio, as well," Jane pointed out.

"I know. Tom was so intent on that literature course he

*Glenna Finley*

was taking that he forgot everybody isn't conversant with seventeenth-century poets."

"That's putting it mildly," she said, smiling. "You were the exception."

"And Josh. He'd identified the source, but he hadn't gotten around to identifying Tom with it. Given more time, I think he would have; I don't underestimate his intelligence." When Jane didn't respond, Hall sighed softly and went on. "If we'd known about the—er—alliance between Anita and Tom, the whole thing would have been obvious. Incidentally, I've transferred that young woman over to the domestic music library."

"For which Señora Forcada will be duly grateful," Jane said with some irony.

"Probably. I was just taking the easy way out. The head of the network library is a sixty-year-old woman who expects a great deal of work in return for a weekly paycheck."

Jane started to laugh. "If I know Anita, that won't last long. She'll be looking for new fields to conquer—or a new announcer."

"Unfortunately, it's a little late for that," Hall said, taking another swallow of coffee. "Now that Tom has a more lucid outlook, he realizes the girl wasn't worth it. But try telling that to a prosecuting attorney or a jury."

There was a silence between them after that, each intent on his own thoughts. Figaro ambled into the kitchen in the middle of it and approached his empty dish beside the refrigerator. He explored it with an inquisitive nose before looking at Jane hopefully.

"Not a chance, my friend," she told him. "Not another morsel until your dinnertime."

The black and white cat bestowed a dispassionate stare

164

that would have withered a less determined custodian. Then he settled purposefully by the feeding dish.

"What are you going to do with that animal?" Hall wanted to know. "Does your landlady want him shipped to her in Maine or left with a vet here?"

"She's making up her mind." Jane chewed uneasily on her lower lip as she watched the quiet cat. "Fig made the mistake of nipping Madame's ankle the day she left town and she's still annoyed about it. I just hope she doesn't make any rash decisions."

"Well, at least it's something new for you to worry about."

Jane wrinkled her nose at him. "I'll work at not being neurotic if it bothers you. Besides, I shouldn't be worrying about Fig—I should be thinking of Madame's poor ankle."

"No doubt." Hall pushed his chair back. "I have to be going. Things have stacked up since I've been out of the office. I hadn't realized how much help Josh had been. Frankly, I wish his appointment to the division had been permanent."

"There may be hope yet," Jane said, keeping her voice level. "I don't think he's decided on his future plans. You'll probably feel better when all this trouble of Tom's has been resolved."

Hall rubbed his forehead as if it ached when he confessed, "I would—if I didn't feel so guilty."

"That's absurd," she began.

"No, not really." He hesitated, and then went on almost reluctantly. "You see, Tom told me about his sister some time ago. She's been in a mental hospital in New Jersey for years."

Jane stared in disbelief. "I didn't know that was the

problem. I just assumed she had a chronic physical disability."

"We can't blame Tom for not spelling it out. The heredity angle bothered him terribly. Maybe the worry was enough to tip him momentarily over the edge. I saw that he was getting more depressed every day, but I just blamed his college courses. Things were in a turmoil at work over the congressional appropriation and pressure from the network side, so I'm afraid I didn't give Tom's troubles more than a passing thought."

"Now look here," Jane said in a firm tone. "You'll have to stop flailing yourself. If you keep on this way, we'll both be neurotics together. At least *I* don't have illusions of grandeur. I still don't see how you could have changed what happened."

"Well, usually I don't miss out on the departmental gossip. If I'd known of his relationship with Anita . . ."

"No way. I'll bet that Anita was darned careful to keep that dark. She knew what would happen if you'd learned he was paying the rent."

Fred Hall managed a thin smile. "You do wonders for my morale. I must confess an emotional triangle was the furthest thing from my mind when Emilio was attacked. I told Lieutenant Nolan there had to be a political motivation."

"Join the party," Jane confessed sheepishly. "And since Horrie and Emilio were on opposite sides of the political arena, I thought your production chief knew more than he was telling."

"Don't tell me you suspected Horrie Cole?" Hall said, scandalized.

"Now you make me feel like an informer. I didn't think he'd hit poor Emilio over the head, but Horrie's been so upset lately . . ."

"He returned to normal earlier today," Hall said with a chuckle. "Madge reported that Mrs. Cole is now in the maternity ward. Apparently she had to drive herself there after Horrie nearly rammed the back of a bread truck and a patrol car on the way."

"Good for Mrs. Cole! I hope Horrie stays clear until the baby arrives or he'll disgrace himself completely by keeling over in the labor ward."

Hall nodded. "He's an emotional fellow, but a splendid production chief nonetheless."

Jane reached over to pat Hall's hand atop the table. "Uncle Fred, you couldn't be disloyal if you worked at it twenty-four hours a day! Horrie will probably make line graphs on everything that new baby will do—including how many times he burps. But the Cole family will be fine, and I officially apologize for ever thinking that such a splendid man might have conked Emilio over the head."

"Now you're teasing," Hall said, "and I refuse to humor you. I knew all along that Horrie was emotional—but sound underneath."

"But what made you suspect Tomás?" Unconsciously Jane reverted to the traffic manager's Spanish name.

"Actually you started my thoughts along that line," Hall admitted. "You said something about the 'idiot prowler' here in your apartment. Suddenly it occurred to me that the person responsible for our troubles might be mentally deranged. Of course, I knew about the history of mental instability in Tom's family, and I'd been puzzled over his appearance on my doorstep that morning. He suggested stopping in here for coffee."

She looked thoughtful. "It all fits. He'd heard me phone Josh that night and must have wondered how much I remembered. Actually, he was as safe as houses if he'd only known. As a detective, I'd make a good plumber."

"That's a putdown which I don't believe."

"No, really, I still don't know why he ransacked the place that night."

"The script," Fred Hall said patiently. "He was after the script. He knew that it had been given to you and he was having second thoughts about the Donne warning. All he had to do was ask around in the department to learn about your date with Mark that night."

"Nothing is sacred in International," she said somewhat bitterly. "He probably could have told everybody what I had for dinner that night."

"Mark informed me that the mahi-mahi was excellent," Hall said with a straight face and then chuckled at her expression. "At any rate, Tom apparently went through your living room looking for the script."

"But he overlooked the cupboard with the cat food where I'd put it," she announced.

There was a pause. Then Hall said mildly, "Well, it was certainly an original hiding place."

"If a trifle scatty."

"I will refrain from the obvious pun. Tom evidently misjudged the time of your return and hid in the bedroom closet when he heard you open the front door."

"I wonder what he would have done if I hadn't obligingly lost consciousness at that point?"

The lines in Hall's forehead deepened. "Don't ask, Jane dear. Don't even ask."

"I think I was almost as upset the next morning," she told him candidly, "when you and Tom 'dropped in' unexpectedly."

"I'd like to have had a picture of you and Josh—it was a tossup as to who looked more distracted. His appearance was a dead giveaway, and you couldn't have acted guiltier if you'd studied for the part. What I first thought was a raging fever was only a permanent blush."

"Very funny." Jane's cheeks took on a suspicion of that same blush. "I suppose it's useless to say that Josh couldn't have been more of a gentleman that night."

"I never for a minute suspected anything else," Hall said promptly.

She stared at him. "Now how should I take that?"

"If you expect an answer, you're out of luck," was his bland reply. "But to get back to what happened, I stopped off at home on the way to the office and picked up my copy of Donne. It was still on my desk when Tom came in later that morning. And that was all that was needed to set him off."

Jane looked skeptical. "It was strange he was walking around carrying that narrow-bladed knife. I'd borrowed it from the shipping department earlier when I was opening a heavy corrugated box and left it in a drawer until I could return it." She chewed on her lip. "I wish now that I'd taken it back."

"My dear, you couldn't keep Tom from all the sharp objects available in the Continental Broadcasting Company. And I don't really believe he intended to use the knife when he lost control and came for me after seeing the Donne on my desk." Hall gestured toward his wounded cheek as he went on. "Otherwise, he could have finished me off after I collapsed."

Jane refrained from mentioning the scene in the corridor later when Tom Carmichael had been well aware of the weapon he had in his grasp. Some things were best forgotten, and that was one of them. Her lips curled in a funny sort of smile. There was going to be quite a list of things she had to forget.

Fred Hall was watching her face. "What are you thinking about now?"

"Nothing important. Remember that Gilbert and Sullivan song—'I got a little list and it never would be missed'?"

"It's a favorite of mine." When she didn't explain further, he shrugged. "I started to leave five minutes ago."

She stopped him when he would have gotten to his feet. "Not yet. There's one more thing. After we found you, Josh told me that you muttered "too much" and "it's hell." It didn't make any sense to me. Did I miss something then, too?"

"If *you*'d heard me, it might have made sense. Although I was fuzzy, I had some idea of what was happening. The trouble was, the Spanish was lost on Josh. I vaguely remember muttering, '*Tomás—es él*'—so you could call for help. Then I guess I blacked out again."

" 'Tom—it is he,' " Jane translated. "You couldn't have been more explicit."

"It was a good idea." His look was whimsical. "Next time, I'll make sure to ask for a translator." As he watched her carry the glass coffee beaker over to the sink, he asked, "Do you plan to spend the rest of the day packing?"

She nodded and linked her arm affectionately in his as they went toward the living room. "I'll have to do it in double-time if I'm ever to get on that train tonight." When she felt something soft brush her ankles, she glanced down. "Fig's keeping close company."

"He's been alone so much lately that he's not going to let you out of sight."

"I think he's just determined to keep an eye on his private chef." Jane frowned as she watched the sturdy figure on the floor. "The Madame's supposed to wire her decision on his future this afternoon. I hope there isn't any problem."

Hall took her firmly by the shoulders and turned her in the direction of the bedroom. "Forget the cat and get to packing. I'll come back to take you to cocktails and dinner before your train and I don't intend to swallow a hamburger in the station concourse because we're late."

She reached up to bestow a swift kiss on his cheek. "You're a dear. I wish I could bribe the bartender to put some knockout drops in your martini so that I could take you along."

Fred Hall cupped her face gently between his palms. "It's a damn shame that I'm not thirty years younger, Janie. The I'd put the knockout drops in *your* martini and keep you here."

# Chapter Ten

☙ ☙ ☙

Jane thought of Fred Hall's affectionate words that evening as she stood at the window of her pullman bedroom and watched his waving figure diminish as the train pulled smoothly out of Penn Station's brightly illuminated concourse and gathered speed.

Inky blackness suddenly replaced the light as the diesel engines plunged into the labyrinth of tunnels connecting midtown Manhattan with the Bronx. Despite this, Jane's slim figure stayed at the window as she stared somberly and unseeingly into the darkness beyond.

Her farewell dinner had been held at a celebrated French restaurant on East Fifty-third street, where the sauce Béarnaise was almost as good as the Chateaubriand. If the occasion had seemed more like a wake than a gala at times, it was because her facade had slipped, revealing her true feelings rather than the flip exterior.

The most cheery part of the cocktail hour had been an

enthusiastic toast to young Horatio Cole, who had weighed in at the hospital at seven pounds six ounces earlier in the afternoon.

"Horatio!" Jane had cringed when told of the arrival. "How could his parents saddle an innocent babe with that name? It must have sentimental associations for them."

"Sentimental, my hat!" Hall had scoffed. "Practical is the operative word. There's a wealthy Greatuncle Horatio in the suburbs who's so pleased with the honor that he's hurrying out to change his will."

Jane started to laugh. "Never underestimate Horrie Cole. I made that mistake earlier—I should have known by now."

Fred Hall nodded as he retrieved the olive from his martini and bit into it. After he'd swallowed and used his napkin, he added, "Incidentally, Horrie sent a special message to you. Apparently he discovered that he'd left his stopwatch at home when they finally arrived at the hospital, so he said that all your practice was in vain. However, he hopes he can use it on the next one. Does that make sense?"

"Not much," she said, still laughing, "but I know what he meant. Tell Horrie for me that by the time the fourth arrives, he should be qualified to write an article for the journal of the American Medical Association." As she fingered the stem of her cocktail glass, she added, "I'll get a present for young Horatio tomorrow in Montreal and have it mailed."

"I'll pass the word along." Hall cast an appreciative glance at her across the table. "That spray of orchids looks very pretty. Did they come from anyone I know?"

"Mark Jamieson. They arrived by messenger just before I left the apartment. I'm sorry to have missed saying good-bye to him in person." She didn't mention that

Mark's card tucked in the flowers had merely said "Expect me as your first house guest." It indicated that he was hoping to continue their acquaintance even if he had to cross the country to do it.

Which was certainly different from another member of the network staff that she could have mentioned. No one in the entire International Division even had news of Josh Blake's present whereabouts, let alone what he planned to do in the future.

And now, Jane thought grimly as she left the window and sat in a chair in the spacious double bedroom, she had all the time in the world to think about it. At least, there was certainly nothing else to do for the next five days en route home. Endless hours of solitude to reflect on how much she loved him and to acknowledge that he'd be impossible to forget no matter how far she traveled. For the first time, the prospect of working abroad loomed as an escape rather than a welcome challenge. She rested her head against the chair back and closed her eyes against the stinging tears that filled them.

A peremptory summons from the buzzer on the compartment door jolted her from her reverie a few minutes later. She quickly searched for a handkerchief in the pocket of her cinnamon velour jacket and dabbed at her wet face. The buzzer sounded again, insistently it seemed.

"Just a minute," she choked out. "I'm coming."

As she reached the door and pulled it open, the train chose to head for another point of the compass. Desperately Jane grabbed for the jamb, missed it as she lost her balance, and catapulted into the corridor.

"Oooh!" Her startled exclamation was smothered as she came up against the shoulder of a dark blue blazer.

"Honestly, my girl," said a well-remembered voice

close to her ear, "sometimes I don't think you should be let outside without a keeper."

Jane froze where she was, noting dazedly that the firm masculine grip which held her hadn't slackened one iota. Her captor seemed content to savor the enchanted moment as well.

Then she pushed back from the comforting shoulder and looked up with appealing candor into his intent glance. "I suppose you're right. Are you—" her words were very soft—"are you applying for the job?"

"You're damned right I am," said Josh Blake just before he bent his head and kissed her.

There was a considerable interval after that before she struggled to regain her senses. During that time she discovered that Josh's vaunted sophistication dissolved along with her resistance as the embrace deepened. When she finally managed to surface, she could hear his heart thudding forcefully and his narrowed glance was dark with need. She hastily lowered her own gaze, knowing that it was equally revealing.

Under the circumstances, it seemed prudent to pull back, but when she tried, Josh merely relaxed his clasp without dropping his arms. Blushing under his amused scrutiny, she managed to say, "This is very nice, but I'd think we'd better talk, too."

"In a minute," he agreed, resting his cheek against the top of her head, as if needing to hold her close for a moment longer. Then he took a deep breath, saying, "I didn't think this day would ever come." That must have triggered a memory because he put her from him an instant later to growl, "Especially after those parting remarks of yours on the sidewalk in front of Continental. They should have been tied with purple ribbon and buried in a deep hole."

"I know." Jane suddenly became conscious of more than one interested passerby in the narrow train corridor. "If we keep standing out here, they'll build a fence around us and charge admission for the show. Let's go in and close the door."

"That's fine with me." He took her elbow and steered her onto the broad padded bench seat before firmly closing the corridor door. "Now then," he said, leaning against it and folding his arms across his chest. "First things first. Are you really feeling okay again?"

"Fine, thanks." She observed him warily, remembering his absence of the past days. "Most anyone at International could have told you that if you'd checked."

"I checked, my love. Every damn day." He gave her a slow, slanted grin. "But I wanted to hear it from you, all the same. Otherwise, I'd have to change my tactics, and God knows, I've had a bad enough time just getting here for the final scene."

"You'll have to clue me in. I don't know what you mean." Jane tried to keep her voice casual but even being in the same room with Josh sent her pulse rate skyrocketing.

"Just that this has been a dastardly plot to get us on the same train," he said calmly, his tall body swaying with the motion of the sleeper. "Some time before we get to Montreal, I mean to convince you to marry me."

A flood of color covered Jane's delicate cheekbones as she solemnly checked the watch on her wrist. "You've accomplished that before we've even left the Bronx and we still have twelve hours before Montreal, Mr. Blake. What shall we talk about now?"

Josh's jaw sagged perceptibly as he stared at her sitting primly on the bench and then he collapsed beside her with a delighted chuckle. "You're a witch," he said, putting his arm around her shoulders and smoothing her hair as she rested her head against his chest. "But a delightful one and I'll forgive you this time because you have a double bedroom. I'd hate like the devil to try any courting in that broom closet of a roomette that Mark reserved for me." He gently tucked a silky strand behind her ear. "I wonder if he was being a sore loser."

"Mark got your reservation?" She tried to raise her head to look up but Josh pulled her back firmly.

"Uh-huh. You can have some breathing room a little later. Just now, I want my arms around you," he said, not as fiercely as he supposed because his lips were partially buried in her hair. "Until five o'clock this afternoon, I was on an airplane coming back from Seattle. And the reason for that, my lovely, was a consultation with your father." He tried to remain stern as she pulled upright at that and stared at him, her eyes agleam with surprise and delight. He couldn't resist her appealing expression, though, and his own eyes mellowed with laughter as he went on. "I have an idea that he thought I was completely balmy for taking a jet back to New York when I could have waited for you out there with a fishing pole in my hand. Other than that, he's all for us."

"Umm—I'm glad."

"So am I. I was able to keep in touch with Mark while I was away. He told me everything that was going on here."

"So that's what he meant by his card," she murmured, before going on to explain. "He sent a gorgeous spray of orchids this afternoon."

Josh's expression was compassionate as he nodded. "I imagine Mark decided that if he couldn't have you, I was probably better than a total stranger. Maybe we can make it up to him."

"I hope so." Jane bit her lip, unsure of how to phrase her next comment. "Josh, what about Ellen?"

"I've known Ellen and her family for years," he replied, choosing his words with care. "When she started getting matrimonial ideas, I had to be diplomatic in turning her down. Otherwise, it would have been difficult all around."

"I can see that, but when I heard she'd gone to Washington with you, it was the final blow."

"Dearest, will you listen to me? Ellen went to Washington with her father," Josh said definitely. "Other than joining them for a cup of coffee on the plane, I didn't run into them again. It wasn't surprising," he added with wry humor. "I announced that I was going to Los Angeles and then I was traveling on to the Northwest to try and get your father's consent to our marriage. That did the trick. After that, Ellen could only offer her congratulations."

Jane felt a moment's sympathy for the other woman before she subsided happily onto Josh's chest again. "You're marvelous," she said. "I've always thought so. . . ."

His burst of laughter cut into her declaration. "Most of the time," he announced wryly, "you've hid your admiration very nicely."

"I was afraid to do anything else." There was no disguising the truth in her tone. "You were completely out of reach. It never occurred to me that you could . . ."

"Love you?" His arms tightened. "Well, that's where you were wrong. I think I knew it that very first day when you had me on my knees under the filing cabinet." He dropped a quick kiss on her lips as she started to protest. "Now, my sweet idiot, you can stop underestimating your powers. If you like, I'll even get down on my knees again—so you can tell our grandchildren that the formalities were properly observed."

"Now who's being silly?"

"You mean I can skip that part?" He brushed his lips caressingly under her ear. "Okay. Would you be interested in knowing that your future husband has been offered a job to head the legal department in Continental's western division?"

"Josh—that's wonderful!"

He squinted down at her, a worried look suddenly on his face. "Does the idea of a few years in southern California sound as promising as working abroad? If it doesn't, I can try for an overseas assignment. I've had some offers in Washington."

"Oh, darling." Her expression was shy but determined as her eyes met his. "Any place with you sounds absolutely marvelous."

For a moment, he was incapable of answering. Then he said roughly, "Fair enough. We'll accept the Continental job and see how it goes for a year or so. If it doesn't work out, we can always give the Foreign Service a whirl. But that's enough of serious topics," he said, stretching his long legs over to the luggage stacked against the wall. "I suppose most of tomorrow will be used up trying to get married in Montreal. Honestly, Janie my girl, with all the United States to get married in, why you had to be difficult and choose Canada, I'll never understand. At least, a honeymoon in Banff should be terrific . . ." He broke off to give a yelp of sudden pain as he bent to clutch his ankle. "What the hell!"

He was staring in horror then—at a black and white paw stretching out through the coarse wire screen of a cat carrier on the floor. A set of sharp talons sank into the bedroom carpet suggestively, as if to compensate for the loss of a human target. From inside the carrier, Figaro's yellow eyes surveyed them. Then he yawned—a long, bored, feline yawn. Obviously he wasn't entranced by what he saw.

"Jane—you didn't—you couldn't—" For the first time in some thirty years, Josh Blake was bereft of words.

"Darling, I couldn't help it." Jane looked beautiful even in her anxiety as she appealed to him. "Madame Trimpani wired this afternoon to say she couldn't take care of Fig any longer. I was supposed to send him to a vet and have him put to sleep." She swallowed with difficulty. "I just couldn't do it, Josh. Can't we work something out? There must be cat trainers who can teach him not to bite you. Darling, it *is* all right, isn't it?"

Josh let his glance linger on her face, as if savoring the abundance of love he saw there. "It will be fine, darling," he assured her. "I'll manage him—starting right now." He leaned over and grasped the cat carrier, turning it firmly toward the bench. "Okay, chum," he said, addressing the occupant. "Now hear this. You can help celebrate the engagement but don't plan on making up a threesome for the honeymoon. Later on, we'll work out the ground rules. Now, go to sleep."

The big black and white cat stared calmly up at him. Then he let out a contented rumble and, tucking his paws under his chest, closed his eyes obediently.

Josh stared in amazement. "Jane! Did you see that?"

"Yes, dear." Quite naturally, her arms stole around his neck.

Josh promptly forgot about everything else as he felt her soft cheek brush past his chin. He tilted her head and bent to kiss her again.

Jane had just an instant to think how different it was from that other kiss the week before, when she'd thought he was going out of her life forever. There was none of that leashed violence in him now. The only undercurrent between them just then was passion—barely held in check. She felt it flare as his hands moved to caress her and she shivered, trying desperately to cling to her last remnant of sanity.

"It's all right, darling." Josh's voice sounded uneven in her ear, but there was laughter in it, too. "I just thought we'd try one of Horrie's time and motion studies."

Jane knew he was trying to reassure her and she relaxed, forgetting her fears. Forgetting everything except that she loved him with every inch of her being and always would.

She smiled then and her fingers were feather-light in tracing the firm line of his jaw as she whispered, "Exactly what did you prove with your research, Mr. Blake?"

"One sure thing. We'd damned well better get married tomorrow," he announced and reached for her again.

# About the Author

〜 〜 〜

Glenna Finley is a native of Washington State. She earned her degree from Stanford University in Russian Studies and in Speech and Dramatic Arts, with emphasis on radio.

After a stint in radio and publicity work in Seattle, she went to New York City to work for NBC as a producer in its international division. In addition, she worked with the "March of Time" and *Life* magazine.

As a producer, she had her own show about activities in Manhattan, a show that was broadcast to England. The programs were similar to those of the "Voice of America."

Though her life in New York was exciting, she eventually returned to the Northwest where she married. Currently residing in Seattle with her husband, Donald Witte, and their son, she loves to travel, and draws heavily on her travels and experiences for the novels that have been published. Her books for NAL have sold several million copies.

SIGNET Books You'll Enjoy

☐ **BEWARE MY HEART by Glenna Finley.** (#W8217—$1.50)*

☐ **DARE TO LOVE by Glenna Finley.** (#W7491—$1.50)

☐ **LOVE FOR A ROGUE by Glenna Finley.** (#E8741—$1.75)

☐ **THE MARRIAGE MERGER by Glenna Finley.**
(#E8391—$1.75)*

☐ **STORM OF DESIRE by Glenna Finley.** (#E8777—$1.75)

☐ **SURRENDER MY LOVE by Glenna Finley.** (#W7916—$1.50)

☐ **WILDFIRE OF LOVE by Glenna Finley.** (#E8602—$1.75)*

☐ **DECEMBER PASSION by Mark Logan.** (#J8551—$1.95)*

☐ **THE CAPTAIN'S WOMAN by Mark Logan.** (#J7488—$1.95)

☐ **FRENCH KISS by Mark Logan.** (#J7876—$1.95)

☐ **WINTER FIRE by Susannah Leigh.** (#E8680—$2.50)

☐ **GLYNDA by Susannah Leigh.** (#E8548—$2.50)*

☐ **THE WORLD FROM ROUGH STONES by Malcolm Macdonald.** (#E8601—$2.50)

☐ **THE RICH ARE WITH YOU ALWAYS by Malcolm Macdonald.** (#E7682—$2.25)

☐ **SONS OF FORTUNE by Malcolm Macdonald.**
(#E8595—$2.75)*

* Price slightly higher in Canada

To order these titles,
please use coupon on the
last page of this book.

To order these titles,
please use coupon on the
last page of this book.

## Big Bestsellers from SIGNET

\* Price slightly higher in Canada
† Not available in Canada

To order these titles, please

use coupon on next page.

## More Bestsellers from SIGNET

☐ **ROGUE'S MISTRESS** by Constance Gluyas.
(#E8339—$2.25)

☐ **SAVAGE EDEN** by Constance Gluyas. (#E8338—$2.25)
☐ **WOMAN OF FURY** by Constance Gluyas. (#E8075—$2.25)*
☐ **HARVEST OF DESIRE** by Rochelle Larkin.
(#E8771—$2.25)

☐ **TORCHES OF DESIRE** by Rochelle Larkin.
(#E8511—$2.25)*

☐ **MISTRESS OF DESIRE** by Rochelle Larkin.
(#E7964—$2.25)*

☐ **LORD OF RAVENSLEY** by Constance Heaven.
(#E8460—$2.25)†

☐ **THE FIRES OF GLENLOCHY** by Constance Heaven.
(#E7452—$1.75)†

☐ **THE PLACE OF STONES** by Constance Heaven.
(#W7046—$1.50)†

☐ **THE QUEEN & THE GYPSY** by Constance Heaven.
(#J7965—$1.95)†

☐ **EVIE'S ROMAN FORTUNE** by Joanna Bristol.
(#W8616—$1.50)*

☐ **EVIE'S FORTUNE IN PARIS** by Joanna Bristol.
(#W8267—$1.50)*

☐ **FORTUNES OF EVIE** by Joanna Bristol. (#W7982—$1.50)*
☐ **LOVER'S REUNION** by Arlene Hale.      (#W7771—$1.50)
☐ **A STORMY SEA OF LOVE** by Arlene Hale. (#W7938—$1.50)
☐ **A VOTE FOR LOVE** by Arlene Hale.      (#Y7505—$1.25)

\* Price slightly higher in Canada
† Not available in Canada

---